ELLE HARTFORD

Steady in Love

First published by Phoenix & Kelpie Press 2024

This novel is entirely a work of fiction. The names, characters and incidents portrayed in it are the work of the author's imagination. Any resemblance to actual persons, living or dead, events or localities is entirely coincidental.

First edition

ISBN: 979-8-9893937-3-2

This book was professionally typeset on Reedsy.
Find out more at reedsy.com

Contents

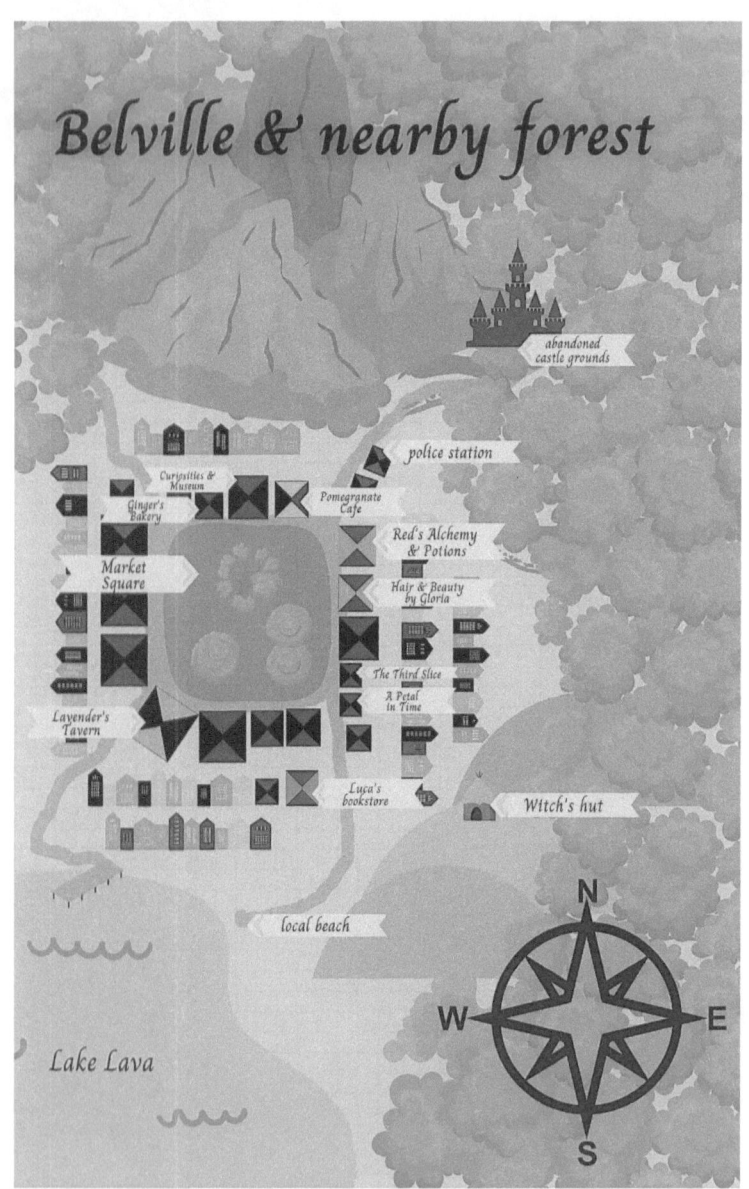

Belville & nearby forest

abandoned castle grounds

police station

Curiosities & Museum

Pomegranate Cafe

Ginger's Bakery

Red's Alchemy & Potions

Market Square

Hair & Beauty by Gloria

The Third Slice

A Petal in Time

Lavender's Tavern

Luca's bookstore

Witch's hut

local beach

N
W E
S

Lake Lava

Prologue

⚬⚬⚬

Sakura

Here we are, one full year of the Pomegranate Café! Of course, I *must* say "we," because I certainly didn't make it here all by myself. They say starting a business is a lonely endeavor, but making it successful is exactly the opposite, I think.

Anyway, you aren't here for a witch's guide to entrepreneurship, are you? I suspect you'll be wanting to hear all about Magica and her participation in the Spring Fair.

I must admit, I have a soft spot for Ostara. As a holiday, it often gets overlooked. But that was the whole point of the Spring Fair, you understand—to observe Ostara, the traditional celebration of spring, blooming flowers, renewed life, and bunnies with eggs. I've never *quite* understood that last part, but children of all ages go wild for multicolored candy-filled eggs.

Belville, as it turns out, has a very checkered history when it comes to Ostara egg hunts. You'd think such a tiny mountain town, even one full of magical beings, would be a little more sedate—wouldn't you? But people, and towns, can be so deceptive.

Speaking of that, there was one person in town spreading all kinds of stories and stirring things up . . . But you'll be hearing enough from them later. I personally don't have patience for that kind of thing.

For Magica, though, I have plenty of patience. Anyone who will step in with only a few days to spare to help out, *truly* help out, with an event is a blessing. And when it comes to love, such sincerity is a definite step in the right direction. Yes, this little plan has been in the back of my mind for a while, but it came together perfectly.

And let it not be said that I don't give credit where credit is due: Glacial was a great help with this one, too. But that's all I have to say about my stubborn business partner at the moment.

I mean it. Don't ask.

Oh—and if you haven't met Magica yet, don't fret. She's only lived in Belville six months or so now. She showed up on a floating carnival, and *quite* a scandal ensued—not that any of it was Magica's fault. Red has already written down all of those details in one of her "Alchemical Tales." But never mind that. The important thing is, the carnival moved on, Magica settled into small town life in Belville, and soon found she wanted to give something back.

As for the person who would help her achieve her goal—and perhaps a little more—just you wait.

This one's been a long time coming!

One

Silver and Gold

~⚜~

Magica

O h, dear. I have a feeling I should apologize in advance. But then I think, what would Gloria say when she reads this?

Gloria *never* apologizes.

(I'm writing this while I'm on a break at work, and when I told Gloria what I'd written so far, she said "I *do* apologize if there's a need for it. There's just never a need!")

I guess I should back up a little. Gloria is my boss at the hair salon, Hair and Beauty by Gloria. When she hired me last fall, I'd never worked in a salon before. But I had a lot of experience doing makeup for carnival acts, so she said I could try it out. If I learned fast, I could stay.

I know this is supposed to be a story about *me,* but it's easier to write about Gloria. She makes everything seem easy. She's like a force of nature, loud and confident and totally *herself.* Which is extra impressive because she's actually got phoenix magic in her family. So she can blow smoke rings when she's thinking, and her hair is actually phoenix feathers, big shiny red ones that rise straight up above her head. And her skin is this really pretty deep orange and her eyes are really sharp and of course her nails are *always* perfect, painted black.

I know how it sounds. I did have a crush on Gloria back when I first settled in. I can admit it now. That's because now we're friends. A week or so after I'd started she had me stay after work for a moment. She told me "I don't do romance, ever, with anyone. But you're a good person. So you can stay and keep working and I'll teach you everything I know about heat styling, but you won't get anywhere hoping for anything more." At first I was mortified. But part of me, deep down, really needed that honesty. So I stuck around and worked harder than ever. Now we have conversations like this:

"Magica, did you finish the—"

"Yes!"

"Magica, I need more of the lilac conditioner at chair t—"

"I left a refill there this morning!"

"Magica, what was the eye shadow shade we needed to reor—
"

"I did it just now!"

And usually right after I say something, Johann laughs. Johann is the other salon employee, and a really old friend of Gloria's. He mostly sticks to the front desk. He's half vampire, and he always says "Magica, in all my years I've never met anyone so like Gloria that they could beat her to the punch.

And do you know how many years that is?"

But it's a joke, of course. I have no idea how old Johann is. It might not be that many. He and Gloria might be ageless, but they both act like they're in their thirties, definitely no more than a decade older than me.

And anyway, I'm *nothing* like Gloria. She's tall and curvy and totally sure of herself. My friends at the carnival used to tell me my last name must be "Willow" for a reason. Straight and brown as a stick and gray eyes like dried leaves—that's what they meant.

I guess the day I realized that Gloria and Johann didn't see me that way is also the day this story really starts.

It was early spring, and raining so hard outside that the big picture windows at the front of the salon were just silver sheets of water running down. There were no appointments on our calendar, and no one was likely to walk in for a hair treatment. Sometimes on afternoons like that we'd rearrange the stock, or Gloria might send Johann and me home early. But that day, she had a new batch of extra-strength hairspray in. Something Red, the alchemist next door, had been working on. I'd agreed to let her practice with it on my hair, since Johann's was too short.

"I don't know what we ever did before you got here, Magica," Gloria told me while she tried to curl ringlets into my long, limp hair. Some of my ancestors were dryads, tree spirits, so while I can't do any magic, my hair does have vines and tiny leaves interwoven in it. I thought they must make it very hard to style, but Gloria never seemed to mind.

"Suffered. That's what we did," Johann said. He was working on touching up my manicure at the time, which he said was a perk for letting Gloria mess up my hair. Gloria always encouraged us to practice with the salon products, but I could never keep my nails looking good, no matter how hard I tried. I'm too used to using my hands without thinking about it.

"Even your hair would probably look better than mine, though," I told him. I knew by then that when Johann said "suffered," he meant that Gloria would be messing with *his* hair instead of mine. But his wavy black hair was actually pretty nice, aside from being too short to be any good in curls or an updo.

Gloria set down her curling wand and put her hands on her hips. "Why would you say that?"

"Because she always says things like that," Johann said.

I looked from one to the other, confused. If it was something I always did, and yet it was wrong, then—

"Stop," Gloria told me. "I know that look. You're panicking."

"I am not," I said. I definitely was. My throat was tight. "What did I say?"

"Honey." Johann set down my hand and reached out to touch my shoulder. He'd switched from professional to friendly and kind. I always found it surprising when he did that, but it was reassuring too. He said, "There's nothing wrong with you or what you said. We're just surprised every time we realize that you don't see yourself the way we do."

"What?" I looked up at Gloria.

She sighed and picked up her curler again. "When I said we're doing curls, what was your first thought?"

"Curls never stick in my hair," I said promptly. "It's too flat and heavy. It just goes straight again in ten minutes. But, um," I added, as soon as I'd realized what I'd said, "I'm glad you can practice, and maybe with Red's special hairspray—?"

Gloria chuckled and shook her head.

I turned to Johann, who sometimes would translate for her since he knew her so well. He grinned at me. "What she means is, it's not the curls that matter. It's getting to practice on your gorgeous locks rather than my spiky head. And it gives me a chance to put a proper polish on your nails. See?" He held up my fingers. The nails gleamed in a shiny coat tipped with gold sparkles. "Now they can match your hair, too. Don't lie to me: if someone asked you, you'd say your hair was brown, wouldn't you?"

I might. I might have said that when I started writing this. But I know that Johann is right. I never really think about my hair, or my eyes, or my face at all being *mine*. Maybe it comes from being made up in the carnival all the time. But I do know what my eyes look like to others, because I have a sibling—a twin. And I remember his eyes and hair very well. Silver and gold.

"You've been here two seasons now," Gloria said through a set of bobby pins held between her teeth. "Isn't it time to *really* give yourself a new start?"

I couldn't move my head, because she was pinning curls in place. I opened my mouth but nothing came out.

Johann grinned at me sympathetically.

Fortunately before I had to say anything the bell over the front door chimed. Against all odds, a customer had arrived. I wasn't even embarrassed I'd be seen with my hair half done. I was just so grateful for an excuse to change the conversation. Without thinking, I waved at the incoming person, my savior.

It was Officer Thorn.

Two

Spring is Coming

Thorn

L isten, I don't know what that shadow witch told you or what she's expecting, but this isn't going to be some sort of tell-all. The *last* thing criminals in Belville need is a personal glimpse inside policing.

Not that you're a criminal. If you know what's good for you, you aren't.

I'll admit that a lot of this is hardly news, though.

Apparently Red was on to me from the start. That kind of observation is why I recruit her as unofficial assistant whenever there's a big case in town.

There might have been a reason I offered to canvas

Market Square looking for last-minute volunteers for the Pomegranate's Spring Fair. The things I told Sakura and Mel—that I needed to stretch my legs, that I wanted an excuse to look in on everyone, that a little rain never hurt anybody—all those things are *true.* Just maybe not quite as true as the fact that I was especially interested in stopping by the salon.

The last thing a town-wide children's event needed was Gloria's attitude or Johann's enabling, but I thought it might be the kind of thing Magica might like. Maybe it would bring her out of her shell a little. Make her feel welcome in Belville. She'd been around for months, sure, but she rarely came to anything or even stopped by the café, or the tavern, or the police station, though of course there was no need for her to seek *me* out. Not that I would have turned her away. But—

I'm straying from the point. The point is, those meddlers at the Pomegranate Café wanted volunteers for their Spring Fair, and I told them I'd go round with a sign up sheet. And then I went specifically to Gloria's salon.

The *real* point is, I've had a crush on Magica since the moment we met.

When she waved at me as I stepped into the salon, my heart stopped dead in my chest.

But then she saw it was me, and she looked at the floor. Even after six months, that was her usual response to me. I hid a sigh as I hung up my guild-issue raincoat by the door.

"Officer, one would think you were half mermaid, going out in this weather," Johann called out. I'm half *orc* and that's hard to mistake, mind you. Green skin, pointy ears, and usually a head taller than everyone else in the room—that's me.

I never really minded before. I liked being muscled and loud. But Magica's just so dainty. It makes me feel like I have two left feet and two left hands to boot.

"More to the point," Gloria added to her assistant's statement, "you're not due back until after Ostara. Did something go wrong with your hair?"

"Did you break a nail?" Johann chipped in.

I shook out my black hair and flashed my nails at them to answer the question with as little fuss as possible. Magica's nails, I noticed, were decorated with beautiful gold flakes. I only ever did mine plain, so it wouldn't be too noticeable when I inevitably broke one.

"Here on official business," I informed them, looking at the ceiling.

Magica hunched her shoulders.

But Johann, as usual, was amused. "Looking for leaks?"

"No," I muttered. "Looking for *volunteers.*"

"Well, as long as you're not here because you think one of us is a criminal." Gloria stepped out from behind Magica's chair, putting her hand on her hip. She had a temper and she'd been in the lineup for a few crimes in the past, but it always worked out alright. No one could have run that salon better. "What do you need us to volunteer for?"

Not you, I almost said. Caught it at the last minute, though. This really wasn't starting off the way I'd hoped. "The, uh, Spring Fair. Mel and Sakura over at the Pomegranate are in charge of it this year."

"Why don't they just run for town council?" Gloria sniffed.

"They put on a nice event, you have to admit," Johann reminded her.

Mel and Sakura and their dubious assistants, Glacial and Ryuko, *had* interested themselves in town affairs quite a bit in the past year. But I have to admit I didn't mind. It took some pressure off the actual town council, and it was nice to see citizens getting involved.

I stuck to the facts of the case. "Mel's looking for people to run booths of kids' games, help out with the egg hunt, or join the decorating committee. Sakura's running the bake sale and cupcake competition."

"Why isn't Glacial running the baking part?" Johann interjected.

"She's part of the entertainment," I said, scrunching up the sign up paper in one hand.

"A person's allowed to do more than bake," Gloria reminded her assistant.

"I'm just saying, she's so *good* at baking. And she never seems to do much else," he mused.

"Well, maybe this is her chance to branch out," Gloria replied.

There was a pause. I wanted to make a comment about *branching out* and spring and things blooming, that sort of thing. But the pun just wouldn't come. That happened a lot around Magica.

For her part, Magica seemed to be thinking something over. She lifted her head a little, shaking out gorgeous deep gold curls as she spoke. "Um—what is the entertainment?"

Gloria and Johann looked at me. I realized they didn't know, and they were waiting for me to answer.

"Glacial's running a kind of talent show," I said, my normally deep voice coming out a little creaky. "She thought it'd be fun for the kids. Give 'em a chance to show off and all that. And—ah—she wanted some adult acts, too. Not adult in content, I mean, but some adults, that could put on acts, not necessarily acting, just something to inspire the kids."

Johann and Gloria kept looking at me until I crossed my arms and looked away. Magica was looking at the salon counter in front of her.

"Acrobatics are a talent," Johann remarked after a moment.

"I'm sure the stage could be arranged properly," Gloria added.

"We could do anything you want," I said as soon as I realized what they were after.

Magica looked up. Hope dawned. "Yes—it wouldn't be hard to set things up," she said softly.

"You'll do it?" I asked.

She met my eyes for the first time. "You can put my name down—yes. I'll do it."

"And you'll go talk to Glacial and the rest of them this evening," Johann added.

"This afternoon," Gloria corrected. "This is worth a little time off."

"Perfect," I said, holding out the paper for her to sign. "This'll be amazing. It's going to be a really good show. Glacial and them are working really hard. They'll be so glad to hear. They've got sponsors and everything, even a special appearance by the golden goose. But you'll be the best act there."

Magica had barely written her name down before she pulled her hand back, avoiding my gaze again. I cursed myself. I'd over done it!

Gloria and Johann insisted on signing up too. Gloria for the bake sale, and Johann as stage assistance for the talent show. Three new signatures on my sheet and I'd only been to one business so far.

Even so, as I walked out, I could have cried.

Three

Delicate

Magica

The moment I agreed to help with the Spring Fair, I regretted it. I don't think Officer Thorn noticed, but Johann and Gloria definitely did. As soon as we were alone in the salon again, they both turned to stare at me in the mirror.

Johann, who'd stood up to sign up for the fair and then see Officer Thorn out, was the first to say something. "What was all that?"

"All what?" I shifted uncomfortably in the salon chair as I looked at their reflections.

"Are you ever going to talk to Thorn?" Gloria asked.

I would say I blanched, but my brown skin doesn't change

color much. It was more a feeling of tightness across my face and shoulders as I averted my gaze.

"Magica, honey," Johann said as he nudged my arm, "you really don't have to be scared about it."

"I'm not scared!" My voice ended in a squeak. My mind was racing. I couldn't figure out how they'd figured it out . . .

"We're just teasing you," Gloria added.

I looked up, confused. This didn't seem like the kind of thing they would tease me about. Normally, Johann and Gloria were really nice and supportive.

He must have seen the look in my face, because now Johann sounded concerned. "What did you think we were talking about?"

"You didn't mean—the goose man?" I asked, more confused than before. I didn't want to say his name.

"Ick, no," Gloria said. She waved one hand dismissively. "There's another one just trying to worm his way into everything in town. At least Saki *lived* here before she started messing with everyone's love life."

"Most people in town would love him to meddle in their lives a bit. No one could turn down free gold," Johann pointed out.

"Then go out and find your own fairy tale goose, I say. There's no need for all this hanging on his every word," Gloria replied. They were now talking over my head.

"Like there's a golden goose around every corner, sure," Johann argued playfully. "I'm just saying, you can't blame them."

"No, but I—"

"You're just jealous no one asked *you* to sponsor the talent show," he added, interrupting Gloria's response.

"Someone *did* just ask me to donate. They just asked for time, not money," Gloria retorted. "But anyway. Why would you think we meant him, Magica?"

Because you just did *talk about him?* I sighed. I didn't want to say anything, and I wasn't mad at them. It was just frustrating to hear about him all the time. Everyone in town was talking about the golden goose and the man who'd brought it into town. I couldn't even get a slice of pizza any more without hearing his name.

Johann came around the chair and sat against the counter instead, looking directly at me. "Are you okay?"

"I'm fine," I said. It took me a minute to find my voice, though.

They exchanged a look over my shoulder—I knew what it meant: *that's an obvious lie.* But they were both too nice to call me out on it. I realized that they really hadn't been talking about him earlier, and started to wonder what else they could have meant about talking to Officer Thorn . . .

"Listen," Johann said kindly. "Aside from everything else, I think it was really brave of you to sign up for the talent show just now. And it's perfectly understandable if you get cold feet about it. The important thing is to follow through as best you can, right?"

I nodded, swallowing hard. "I just wanted to give something back. To Belville."

"I don't know if the whole *town* deserves gratitude," Gloria said, resting her hand on her hip. "But I agree with Johann. It's a good thing to do."

"And bonus, it'll be good for you," Johann added brightly. "This is exactly the kind of thing we were just talking about, isn't it?"

I nodded, although I was still confused about what exactly we'd been talking about earlier.

"So what are you going to do?" Gloria asked, as she began

working on the other half of my hair.

"She's going to be amazing, obviously," Johann said. Since he was done with my nails, he just kept leaning on the counter, watching Gloria twist locks of my hair into curls.

"I meant *specifically*," Gloria told him, with a familiar reprimanding glance. "You must know all kinds of acrobatic routines, right?"

She'd addressed me directly in the mirror, and it startled me out of my wondering and doubts. "Um . . ."

"No need to be modest with us," Johann said encouragingly. He grinned as he added, motioning at Gloria, "You know what *she's* like, after all."

I smiled a little at that. "I *have* done a lot of shows. And we'd change the routine every season. I've trained in a couple different kinds of acrobatics, actually."

"So presumably, you have options," he concluded.

"But are you only used to performing with a partner?" Gloria asked through several bobby pins.

My smile faded. "I did perform mostly with my brother. But I did some routines alone, too."

"Now I'm bummed we missed out on the carnival last summer," Johann said, before I could start to feel too badly. "I bet you were amazing. A twin acrobatic act—how cool is that?"

"I'm sure the act was cool, but the carnival was not," Gloria reminded him a little severely.

"It wasn't the whole carnival that was a problem," I said quickly. "Just—a few people."

We left it at that.

"Anyway, it'll be even better now that you can design your own routine for just you," Johann said.

I was so grateful in that moment that he really thought that. I looked hard at him for a moment, and when he smiled, I smiled back.

"And you know exactly who will be helping with your hair and makeup," Gloria added.

I looked up at her in the mirror, and was surprised to see that my hair was a mass of curls. "No one will even recognize me!"

Johann laughed. "Oh, they'll recognize you."

"I can think of one person in particular," Gloria added, smirking.

"What?" When I met her eyes, blinking, she just grinned wider.

"Never mind," she said. "How about you head over to the Pomegranate and talk to them about the fair while I clean up?"

"I'll come with you," Johann added, hopping off the counter. "It's about time for my afternoon tea."

Gloria gave him a hard time about his afternoon tea habit— as usual—but I was secretly glad he'd decided to come along. We pulled on our boots and raincoats, though he insisted I shouldn't put up my hood. Instead, he offered me one of the salon umbrellas. I'd always thought they were so special, because they were charmed to never leak or turn inside out in the wind. All our customers seemed to think this was pretty normal, but I loved it. After living on a carnival ship my whole life, it was a novelty to think we could go out in a storm—or even go out at all—without getting wet.

We set out with our matching umbrellas. It was a short walk, really: Hair and Beauty by Gloria is near one corner of Market Square, and then there's Red's Alchemy and Potions actually *on* the corner, and then across a diagonal street is the Pomegranate Café. The sound of the rain on the leaves of the trees in the Square was overwhelming. Rainwater pooled around the cobblestones in the road. But there was still something cozy about it, walking over to the tea house with Johann.

I've always thought that the Pomegranate is one of the cutest buildings in Belville, though I've never said so to anyone. Gloria's salon is very nice of course, but really just glass and brick from the outside. And Red's potion store always has very interesting window displays. But the café is painted this lovely deep pink, with white wood trim and shutters, and it's set back just enough that it has a tiny little patio with outdoor chairs and tables and even a place where you can leave or borrow a book. It was the perfect place to sip a lemonade, read a really good new story, and listen to the birds and kids playing in Market Square. I hadn't worked up the courage to do that yet myself, of course, but every time I looked at the café, that's what I thought.

Actually, I hadn't been into the Pomegranate more than two or three times. Usually Johann was happy to take everyone's order from the salon.

This time when we walked in together, it was a little exhilarating. There were people on every chair, sitting at sofas under the front windows, crowded around tables on the second floor balcony. Everyone was talking and laughing and drinking teas that smelled amazing. Towards the back corner of the café, Sakura was practically hidden behind the bakery case and register. She made coffee and tea using shiny machines that lined the back wall. Her bright pink apron seemed to lighten up the whole place.

Johann went right up to the counter, and he beamed at Sakura when she paused to take his order. "My usual, please, in your largest to-go mug. I have to get back to Gloria, but I'm leaving this one in your care," he told her, pointing down at my head.

I blushed. To be heard over the crowd, I nearly had to shout. "Um, hi, Sakura? My name's Magica. We—we were thinking that I should maybe talk to someone about the talent show. For the Ostara fair? But I can come back at a better time . . ."

Sakura leaned her elbows on the polished wood counter and looked me up and down. I'd heard a lot about her, of course. Some people at the salon said she was a shadow witch, which meant she had magical powers but had never gone to an official Witch school and therefore was a rebel and maybe even a reformed evil witch. They said she could see into people's souls.

But that isn't how she *looked* at all. She had bright white hair cut in a perfect bob, and her eyes were sunny sky blue, and her cheeks were rosy, probably from having to make so many drinks to keep up with the demand. She was only an inch or so taller than me. Plus, little ceramic cats dangled from her ears. She didn't look threatening at all.

Of course, every carnival performer knows that sometimes it's best to look the opposite of your part. It adds to the humor. Or the suspense.

"You're here at the perfect time," Sakura decided. "Call me Saki. The person you want to talk to is Glacial. I'll bring her out in just a minute. You want anything while you wait?"

"Um—" I glanced up at Johann. I hadn't been prepared for that question. Silly of me, since we were in a café standing at the register, and yet—

"She'll have cherry blossom matcha. With your best foam art," he said easily.

Sakura grinned. Her grin was lopsided, like maybe it *could* have been evil, but instead it came across as adorable. "I *only* do my best foam art. Coming right up!"

I tugged at one of my new curls, trying to remember if I'd ever had this drink before. But Johann paid and shooed me down along the counter as if this was a normal part of every day.

"You'll love it, trust me," he said. "And I think you're going to love Glacial."

"Mind you don't tell that to a certain someone!" Sakura sang out from behind a row of steaming kettles.

"What was that?" I asked, glancing to Johann for clarification.

"Oh, nothing," he said. It occurred to me then that *his* grin could look a tiny bit evil sometimes, too.

Four

Split Ends

⚬⚬⚬

Thorn

I did my rounds asking for volunteers from the rest of the businesses around the Square. Let it not be said that I don't follow through on my promises.

I ended up back where I'd begun. This time, I went into Red's store, doing my best not to look into the salon.

It didn't look like anyone was there any more, anyway. Gloria probably gave 'em the afternoon off.

I knew Red would be in, though. She *lives* in her potions lab. Technically she lives in the studio apartment above the shop floor, along with her magical dog, William. She thinks I don't respect her as a shopkeeper, or an alchemist, or what have you. That's not true. It's just that alchemists are so useful at being other things, too. They're resourceful.

And resource-full, what with all the alchemical conveniences. Get it?

My puns may have been back, but at the time I was not feeling one hundred percent, I can tell you that. I shoved the potions shop door open and stood on the front mat, shaking water out of every crease in my coat.

William, afore-mentioned magical dog, immediately barked at me. "You're getting rain all over our wares!"

"Then you ought to make them waterproof," I answered. I'm not intimidated by anyone, least of all an overgrown mop of a black sheepdog. Even if he was some kind of high-powered sorcerer's familiar once.

"Too bad nothing in Beyond is Officer Thorn-proof," the dog grumped back at me.

"Keep up that attitude and your shop is going to be customer-proof," I warned him.

"Play nice!" Red's voice floated out from her laboratory, which was behind William and the sales counter, separated from the shop by a wall and an open window. "Also, glass bottles *are* waterproof, so we're fine. And customers don't come out in the rain anyway. I'll be out in just a minute."

While she finished whatever she was doing, I chucked my rain gear to one side and made my way through the rows of potions. There were a few stuffed chairs and a teapot in the right corner, but I didn't feel like being comfortable. Instead I leaned against the counter across from William.

"Slow day?" I asked.

"Unless you're about to drag us into some kind of crime, then yes," he answered from his perch on an old wooden stool.

I cracked a rueful grin at that. A crime might've been a nice distraction. And you'd be hard-pressed to find better backup than Red and William, even if you had your pick of the Police Guild's finest new trainees.

"My guess is she's here to press us into a different kind of service," Red said, emerging from a door behind the counter. She was still pulling off her gloves and lab coat, which she stowed in the back room before locking the lab and joining us. "Rhys was telling me earlier that even he and Daisy have been asked to help with the Spring Fair for Ostara. I was wondering if we should be glad or worried that we haven't been asked too."

"Definitely glad," William said, panting.

"I was getting to it," I told her, trying not to sound defensive. "It's been a long day."

"It's barely three o'clock." Red gave me one of her knowing looks. She does it a lot: raised eyebrow, pursed lips. With her black hair tied back in a ponytail and her lab goggles pushed up over her forehead, she looked like an illustration of the "skeptical scientist" entry in an encyclopedia. "Is there some trouble with the fair?"

I huffed and turned away from the two of them and their identical head-to-one-side curious looks. "The fair's fine."

"She didn't say it was *fair*," I could hear William telling Red. "She's broken."

"I do not *always* make puns, thank you very much," I protested. "Some are just too easy."

"What restraint," Red said. I could tell from her voice she was holding back a laugh. "So, will we be enjoying an acrobatics display at the fair?"

"Yes. Maybe. That isn't the problem." This time I *knew* I sounded defensive.

William snorted.

"Why would you ask that?" I added, crossing my arms across my chest.

"No reason, I guess," Red said. She was chuckling, curse her. But then she walked around the counter to my side, and hopped up to sit next to me. "So, how's volunteer collection been going?"

"Shouldn't you be mooning over your bookseller or something?" I asked.

"Listen, you're the one who showed up here," she replied. "We're just trying to help. Right, William?"

"*I'm* trying to live my afternoon in peace," the dog retorted.

"Neither one of you is helping very much," I declared.

"Then tell us what you want," William demanded. I could tell from his voice he was getting tetchy for real this time.

I sighed. Truth was, I didn't really know what I wanted. Maybe I *had* been hoping that a crime would show up and distract me as soon as I entered their shop.

Red sighed, too, but hers was a more gentle sound. "It's probably no use pointing out that this isn't like you, is it? And encouraging you to just be yourself?"

"Being herself is the problem," William chipped in.

Red's reprimand was instant. "*William!*"

"No, it's fine. For once, I agree with the dog," I admitted.

"I didn't mean it like that," he insisted. I glanced over my shoulder at him, and he wagged his fluffy tail. "There's nothing wrong with *you*. Mostly. It's just that you're too stubborn. You're too used to pining silently, so now you won't go *say* something."

Red looked up at me speculatively. "You know, he might be right about that. And he did just admit that there's nothing wrong with you. That's big coming from him."

"*Mostly,*" he reminded her.

I sighed again, louder this time. "Whether he's right or not isn't much use now."

"Why not?" Red asked.

"I promised Sakura and Mel that *I'd* help with the fair, too," I confessed.

Red straightened. "So? That's perfect. You can practice together, and—"

"No, no. I promised I'd donate some boughs from the family farm. Cherry blossoms to go along with the decorations, and all that. Ma's even bringing over a sapling to dedicate to the town, and—"

Just as I was gaining steam, they interrupted me. This is how you know neither Red nor William ever received any formal training in investigation. Never interrupt a suspect!

"I still don't see why this is a problem," Red was saying.

"Hold on," William said over us both. "Your family grows *cherry* trees?"

I looked over my shoulder again, this time to frown at him. "What? Orcs can't like nice things?"

Red tugged her ponytail over her mouth, and I shifted to glare at her too. "Don't you say anything. There's no pun in that!"

"None," she agreed, though her smile wasn't very serious. "A cherry orchard sounds very nice, and that's really kind of your family. They haven't visited since All Hallows, right?"

"No," I agreed, albeit grumpily. "And this time it's just Ma. But that makes it worse. There'll be no one to distract her."

Red's smile was now a massive grin. "You're going to try to hide this from her, aren't you?"

"Worked last fall," I muttered, wishing the floor would just swallow me up already."

William *woof*ed in amusement. "Your hiding days are over."

"Still not helping!" I reminded the room at large.

"It's going to be fine," Red said, laying one hand on my arm. "And look at it this way. The fair is a perfect chance for your mother to meet her, and—"

"NOT HELPING." I pushed off the counter and began pacing the center aisle of the shop. Much as I loved my Ma, picturing her and Magica together was enough to start me shaking like a leaf.

"Fine," Red said, still smiling. "Well, if you insist on finding something else to think about, maybe you'll be interested in the test I was just running. I got my hands on a bit of eggshell from that golden goose—"

"I checked into that already," I said absently, shaking my hair off my shoulders. "He's got all the right paperwork. It checks out."

"Paperwork is one thing, but free gold is another," Red said. She was getting her "skeptical scientist" look again, and I could sense a lecture. "I know there've always been tales about 'golden' geese, but there's no way to actually *create* gold, except the natural way, which does *not* involve fowl. Alchemists have been trying for centuries—"

I paced faster, but still couldn't think of anything but Magica. Would she think I was a country dolt, backward, because I grew up on a farm? Would she think it was weird my mother was coming to the fair? Was there any way possible I could keep them apart?

Not with Red focused on her wild goose chase, there wasn't. I needed all hands on deck.

"Let's not go looking for problems," I decided. "We have

enough to deal with already."

"Didn't you come here looking for a problem?" William pointed out.

"*You're* a problem," I retorted without thinking about it.

When I realized what I'd done, I opened my mouth to apologize. To admit I'd gone too far. But looking between William and Red, neither one looked like they'd taken it to heart. Red looked sympathetic, and William was totally unfazed. They were so normal and understanding.

I turned on my heel and fled the store.

Five

Change My Mind

Magica

After Johann and I picked up our drinks from the end of the counter, he led the way to an old couch in the far corner, underneath one of the front windows. A group of forest elves stood up from it just a second before, and Johann practically threw himself across it while they were still pulling on their rain ponchos.

"Gotta move fast around here," he said to me, grinning as he made room so that I could sit down too.

"I knew the Pomegranate was popular, but not *this* popular," I agreed. I did my best not to make eye contact with the couple sitting on the loveseat across from us. They were even younger than I was . . .

"It's the rain," Johann said. He always sounded so confident, like he knew every answer. I don't think it's because he's lived a long life or anything like that. I was about to ask him how he always sounded so self-assured, but then he added, "Wish me luck going back out into it. Here's hoping I make it to the salon without drowning."

"You're not staying?" I asked, trying not to sound as alarmed as I felt.

"Gloria can't be left alone in the salon for too long. You know what happened last time," he told me. I had to admit he was right. Even though the salon was Gloria's, she tended to get itchy feet if she had too much time on her hands. During a winter blizzard, we'd come in one morning to discover that she'd totally upended the shampoo collection during the previous afternoon when she'd told us to go home. So Johann's explanation made sense, but it didn't make me feel any better. He nudged me as he went on, "I just wanted to make sure you got a good seat. Now you're settled, and it'll probably only be a moment before Glacial finds you. Just you wait."

I sighed. I've never been too good at waiting.

But I also knew Johann had really gone out of his way to be kind to me. I put on my best smile and thanked him as he left. As he headed for the door, I couldn't help but notice that the couple on the other side of the coffee table were basically on top of each other now.

I wonder if Sakura has a policy about PDA . . . But I was much more preoccupied wondering about Glacial. I'd never even seen her. Would she be a new best friend, as Johann seemed to think? It seemed more likely that she'd be a super talented and high-performing person with no time for my foibles. She might not even notice me, sitting hunched over in a far corner.

Should I have stayed at the counter? It was probably a waste of her time, making her look for me. On the other hand, if she never found me, then eventually I could leave, and maybe forget about the whole talent show . . .

"Do you like it?"

I startled, making my drink slosh around the sides of its pink ceramic mug. "I'm so sorry!"

"It's fine. Do you like the tea?"

When my thoughts finally settled down and I focused on this new person, at first all I noticed were her eyes. One was lavender, one was pale blue. I think I was staring. "The tea?" I repeated, dazed.

"The tea," she confirmed.

I looked back down at my cup. This was not at all the conversation I'd expected to have, and it took me a minute to marshal my words. I ran my fingers over the ridges in the handmade mug. "Um, I've never had it before. But yes, I do. I don't think I would have thought to order it. It was my coworker Johann's idea."

"It's not too floral?"

I paused. Could something be too floral? "Um, no? I like it. I think it's nice."

The woman with mismatched eyes nodded, and then rose. She'd been sitting right next to me, and I'd been so nervous I hardly noticed anything about her. As she stood up in front of me, I could see she had a white tale, almost like a panther's but covered in scales. She was wearing a white tank top and denim shorts, a strangely out-of-place outfit for a rainstorm in early spring—and when she faced me again, I realized it had been covered up before. She was wearing a Pomegranate Café apron.

"Wait!" I cried. Because of the noise in the café, I was too loud. She turned and looked down at me with her hand on her hip and it reminded me of Gloria. I cleared my throat. "I just realized. Are you Glacial?"

"Yes," she said, her tail twitching behind her. It barely missed the vase of flowers on the coffee table. Like Sakura, she was short—like me.

"I think I'm supposed to be meeting with you?" I said.

"That's what Saki said," Glacial agreed.

But . . . she didn't seem very interested in meeting. Why had she already gotten up to leave? I gripped my pink mug tighter. "Um, is this a bad time?"

Glacial kept looking at me. Her skin was pale blue, like her one eye. It's not unusual to have skin of any color in Beyond, but for some reason it made me think of Officer Thorn. I pushed that thought aside and tried to focus. Glacial's hair was lavender, pulled back in pigtails. She had large eyes and a small nose, smudged with flour. How had I not immediately known this was Glacial, the baker? She looked exactly like what everyone said she was. But her voice was almost too deep for her when she spoke. "I'm going to be scary no matter what time it is."

I startled again, and swallowed. "What?"

Her eyes narrowed a little as she watched me. I had a feeling I wasn't fooling her about anything. "I scare you. I don't think I'm really the person you want to talk to."

"But I was just startled. It was just because I was—I didn't expect anyone to ask about the tea," I said, knowing it sounded lame, because I'd literally been waiting for her.

"It's fine," she said again, shrugging one shoulder. "I'm used to it. I'm sure you'd rather talk to Saki."

I blinked. Everything about Glacial was pastel except her pomegranate-red apron. She was probably even smaller than me, especially since I'd gained a little weight since living in Belville. Was she really that scary?

Get a grip on yourself, I thought. I looked at her again, this time trying to think of what I'd see if I was sizing her up as a fellow performer at the carnival. She was definitely fit. I'd never tried baking, but I doubted most bakers needed that many shoulder muscles. *Officer Thorn is probably even more fit under her uniform.* The thought came up and I swatted it away. Now that I was looking more carefully, I noticed a scar along Glacial's left cheek and small white scales lining the bones in her hands, like armor. The same scales traced up her arms, interlaced with more scars.

The only people I'd ever met with that many scars were the occasional security guards we'd hire at the carnival when we were in a really busy port.

"Wait," I decided, as she turned to leave again. This time when she looked back, I took a deep breath and said, "I'm not scared of you. I was just startled. It happens a lot. But I want to—I want to talk to you about the talent show."

Glacial set both her hands on her hips. "You're sure?"

I nodded. "You don't have to have Sakura give me a different job at the fair. Unless you don't think I would be good in the talent show . . ."

She sat without looking at me, and I realized that she'd probably sized me up the moment she first saw me. "Saki told me you used to be a carnival acrobat. We don't have anything like that in the show yet."

Suddenly I was dying to ask what *she* would do in the talent show. But I thought it might be better not to ask that yet. "I can do whatever kind of show you want. Just a few minutes, or a whole set, or aerial hoop, or if we could rig up silks, they wouldn't even have to be on the stage. Just in the trees nearby would be good," I said.

Glacial shifted. She'd been staring at my mug, but now she looked at me from the corner of her eye. For the first time, she smiled a little. "You can do whatever you want. You don't have to prove anything to me."

"But . . . it *is* a talent show," I pointed out.

"No one's judging it. You could do anything and still be part of it." Glacial sat back to look me in the face.

And in that moment, sitting face to face again and really paying attention for the first time, I saw it. Johann was right. I *did* like Glacial. We had something in common. She knew what it was like to feel like you have to constantly *prove* things, and she was trying to create a show where no one else would feel that way.

I smiled at her and saw that she was already grinning back. Before, I'd been worried and a little nervous about the show. Now, it felt more like the old days at the carnival. I could feel some of that confidence that comes from knowing the whole troupe is there with you. *I can do something really cool,* I thought, almost giddy. *I can create my own act, and everyone will see it, and then she'll realize—*

Best not to go *that* far just yet. I refocused and told Glacial, "I'd be really glad to be part of it."

"Then you are." Glacial hesitated, then added with another smile, "Do you need a place to practice?"

"I would *love* one." Until I heard it in my voice, I hadn't known how much I'd missed practicing every day.

While Glacial filled me in about the gym she was setting up

and the timeline for the show, somehow I downed my entire mug of tea. By the time she had to get back to the kitchen, I could feel myself buzzing. Working in the salon was one thing, but the thought of having a show to practice for again had wiped away all my doubts.

I went to the salon to fill in Gloria and Johann, who only had good things to say. Of course Gloria sent me home early so I could start planning—as if I didn't already have several ideas in my head! I thought them over as I walked on through the rain. I wanted to pick something spring-themed for the holiday. I wanted to do all my favorite moves. I wanted to make it really impressive and maybe even a little attractive because *surely* in the audience would have to be—

All my happy thoughts fizzled when I saw the dead rat hanging from my door.

Six

Rats and Mice

Thorn

Needless to say, I wasn't too proud of myself that night after I handed the volunteer sign-up sheet to Sakura and Mel. They met every evening to go over plans for the fair. On a normal day I might have hung around for some intel. But when they started talking about how Magica and Glacial were cooking up an extra-special talent show, I hightailed it out of there.

I don't want you to go thinking I'm a coward. It's *different* when you're the police officer in a town like Belville. I'm the only one there. That's unless there's some trainees hanging around, of course, but at that particular time, there weren't. Thank Justice.

The thing is, when you're the one everyone looks to for keeping peace, you're never off duty. You're *always* the one everyone looks to. It's a responsibility. And I like responsibility just fine, mind you. It'd never been a problem before.

But talking about Magica didn't make me feel very responsible.

I spent that evening hiding out in the station. Belville's police station and living quarters come along with the job. Upkeep, cleaning, keeping open hours—that's all part of the responsibility, too.

I ate my takeout sitting at the station's front desk with my boots up. It's a bad habit. I'll be the first to admit I'm not the coziest of people. But that's *not* because I was raised in a barn, or orchard technically. I just have a lot of other things on my mind.

Not to mention things I try to keep *off* my mind, these days.

It wasn't a very restful night, but I woke up the next morning determined to give the new day a fresh start. Even if it was still raining. The fair was just three days out, which meant Ma was due to show up in a day or two. There was plenty to do before that. All I needed was something to keep me busy, and there were plenty of options.

But when I went to unlock the station door and found Magica standing on the front stoop, my plans ground to a halt.

"Perfect timing. See, I told you the station would be open. You aren't going to make us stand out here in the rain, are you, Officer?"

I hadn't noticed Johann standing behind Magica. Not until he started talking, of course. As they snapped their umbrellas shut and shuffled into the station, he kept talking nonstop.

I stepped back to let them in. Suddenly I was cursing myself for not having gotten up earlier to give the place a good scrub or to go out and grab breakfast. It's not like sleep had done me much good anyway.

"Officer Thorn?" This time it was Magica who spoke.

I snapped to attention. Johann was already sitting in the chair behind the front desk. Magica had lingered by the door. By me.

As I looked down into her eyes, I started to worry. Her hair was pulled back in a messy braid, with little leaves poking through the pattern. She was biting her lip. I cleared my throat. "Is everything okay?"

She hesitated. She'd never held my gaze this long before. But when she shook her head, my heart puddled at my feet.

"It's going to be," I promised. It was barely more than a whisper. "We'll figure it out."

Her eyes widened, and she glanced at Johann.

"That's what I said," he declared. He was hanging his wet scarf off the back of my chair, the scoundrel. "Belville Police Station may be small, but it is mighty. Isn't that so, Officer Thorn?"

"What's happened?" I asked them, shutting the door and pulling up a chair for Magica, then another for me. The station's furniture is sparse, but I try to have good chairs around. If nothing else, they're useful when Red and William end up eating with me while we work on a case.

Johann looked pointedly across the desk at Magica. She was hunched up in her chair, not looking at either of us now. In fact, she was considering the wood paneled wall like it'd said something hurtful.

For my part, I glared at Johann. Couldn't he see he was making things awkward for her? "I take it you're the one who insisted on coming here," I prompted him.

"Magica didn't seem to think it merited a report," he said by way of explanation.

"Everything merits a report," I told her at once. Then I regretted it. "Well, maybe not *everything*. But if something's made you upset, or made you feel unsafe, then you should absolutely report it. We'll handle it."

"You were upset when you came in this morning," Johann added pointedly to Magica. Since he was being helpful for once, I let the interruption slide.

"I—it *was* upsetting," Magica admitted, only glancing briefly between us. "But there's no one—no one to blame, really."

Johann beat me to responding. "Why don't you let the officer be the judge of that?"

She glanced at me one more time, then away. "It was just a silly thing."

"Nothing's too silly," I assured her.

She seemed to think about this for a moment. I wished I had some tea to offer her. But they'd come in right at opening time, and I had nothing. Finally, she spoke again. "When I got home last night, there was a dead rat on my door."

"It was on your *door*?" Johann leaned forward. "You didn't tell us that!"

I glared at him again before focusing on her. "How?"

"It was—the tail was tied around the doorknob," she said uneasily.

"Could you see how it had been killed?" I immediately regretted asking the question, but it had to be done.

"The neck was broken," she said very quietly.

I leaned back and tried to get control of myself. "What happened next?"

"I—I didn't want to leave it there, so I took it down and—buried it," she said. Johann *tsk*ed and she looked up immediately. "Did I do something wrong?"

"It's a perfectly understandable impulse," I said.

"I was just thinking about touching a dead rat, honestly," Johann added.

"I wore gloves, and I washed everything," Magica assured us. "I have some of the rubber gloves we use for dyeing at home. Gloria said I could take some for cleaning."

"I'm glad she did," Johann said.

I thought things through. No evidence to go over at this point, but I didn't doubt Magica for a second. "Where do you live?"

Johann gave me a look, but I ignored it.

"I'm renting a flat from the inn," Magica told me. "Not actually *in* the inn, but a few streets back. Towards the lake."

Of course I knew Lavender had rented her a flat. But I hadn't gone so far as to ask which *one*. As innkeeper and one of Belville's oldest residents, Lavender owned several old houses around town.

"Any housemates?" I asked.

Magica hesitated, then shook her head. "I live on the ground floor. There's an apartment upstairs, I think, but it's been empty."

Winter was not a popular time to visit an alpine town, after all. But that cut out the easiest source of suspects. I resolved to get the full address and check the place out myself later. Maybe someone'd been using the upper floors in secret.

"Any neighbors?" I asked, moving on through my mental list of possible suspects and witnesses.

"There's the owners of A Petal in Time there, right?" Johann inserted helpfully.

Magica nodded slowly. "They live on the corner, maybe two houses down. There's only houses lining the street. A lot of people live there, but I only know some of them. I know there's an old man in the house across the street, but I've never talked to him."

"Kids?" I asked. Knowing the area, I figured there were lots of school-age kids running around there, walking to and from school.

"I do see them walking," Magica said, almost as though she'd read my mind. For a moment she met my eyes again, and I almost smiled at her.

Then Johann interrupted again. "You don't think one of them would have done it as a prank?"

"Doesn't make much sense, since you're hardly new to the neighborhood, and I'm sure you haven't been a inconsiderate neighbor," I said, still focused on Magica. "But it's a possibility. Did it mean anything to you, Magica? Have you ever had anything like that happen before?"

She nodded slowly, then shook her head. "I—not in Belville, I've never had anything like that happen. Once around the holidays someone gave me some Yule cookies, but that's it. That's nothing like this."

It wasn't, and it made my heart ache for her. I wished I'd had the courage to give her the cookies that were still shoved into the back of the icebox in my little kitchen.

"But you do know something about it?" Johann pressed. For once, I had to admit it was good he was present and keeping us on track.

"I don't *know* anything about it," Magica said quickly.

"This morning when you came in you said someone'd sent

you a message," he reminded her, leaning over the desk.

"I just thought that because—" she hesitated, glancing at me. "It's just, something people used to say in the carnival. If you told someone's secret and got them in trouble, then you were a rat."

"You think someone's saying you're a rat?" Johann scrunched up his long nose.

"If that's the case, then this could be a direct threat," I realized, sitting up.

"Um—I don't know if that's what they meant," Magica said. She was clearly alarmed.

"But it could be," Johann insisted.

"It might not have even been meant for me," Magica argued.

"Someone literally stood there and tied it to your door," Johann shot back.

"Maybe they made a mistake—"

"I think I'd make double sure I had the right house if I was about to be messing around with dead rat!"

"Let's stay calm," I said, though to be honest I might have been the most disturbed of any of them. I didn't let it show, though. One look at Magica and I could tell she needed that calm.

So, instead of barging down the door and immediately arresting the entire town, which I *wanted* to do, I remained in my seat and pulled my notebook out of my breast pocket. "Let's go over everything one more time," I said, as gently and as authoritatively as I could manage. "And then we'll discuss how to move forward."

Seven

Other People

Magica

I guess I'd assumed that Officer Thorn might think I was wasting her time with the rat thing. Pranks and messages and things like that happened all the time when I was in the carnival. Maybe not *all* the time, not with the dead animals. But probably everyone would have told me I was being silly.

Not Officer Thorn, though. She was so nice. She's been nice every single time I've seen her. At first I thought it was just that everyone in Belville is nice. But as Gloria has pointed out, that's not necessarily true. No one is as nice as much as Officer Thorn is.

She promised to take a look around the neighborhood and ask some questions, even though I wasn't sure she'd find anything. It made me nervous to think of her going out and maybe wasting her time, but she was really determined. So after a little while, Johann and I went back to the salon.

Between the rat and the rain, Gloria and Johann didn't let me out of their sight all day. I tried telling them not to worry, but it didn't work. And honestly . . . maybe I didn't mind that they were worried. *I* was worried too. Maybe it was bad of me to let them worry in the first place? They could have had a perfectly normal, quiet day if not for me.

I was hoping just to forget about it all by the time we were ready to close the salon. But apparently Officer Thorn hadn't forgotten one bit. She showed up right as Gloria was about to send us home.

"You're headed to the café?" she asked. She always knows things.

I nodded. "Glacial told me she's set up a gym in the lot right behind the café, so I was going to go there and practice."

Officer Thorn frowned. "You won't be alone, will you?"

"No, I think Glacial will be there," I said quickly.

She pulled her hood up over her hair, and I grabbed my bag and opened my new umbrella. For a moment we walked in the rain without speaking. It wasn't as much of a downpour as it had been yesterday—now it was more of a drizzle. I could hear Officer Thorn's boots hitting the cobblestones with each step, and something about the sound was very reassuring.

"I canvassed the neighborhood," she said eventually.

"You didn't have to do that," I told her, stealing a brief glance up to see if she looked annoyed.

"Of course I did." The way she said it wasn't angry, just matter-of-fact. Something about it made me release a breath I hadn't realized I'd been holding. She went on, "No one's saying they

41

saw anything out of the ordinary, but I wouldn't worry about that. A clue will turn up. They always do."

"You don't think—something will happen again, do you?" I asked. "If I'm quiet, and just keep to myself, then there's not any reason for anyone to do something like that again, right?"

Water splashed off of her yellow hood as she shifted to look at me. "No one can say for sure except the perpetrator. Whether or not anything happens, it's not your fault. *You* aren't the one who killed that rat, are you?"

It was a rhetorical question. I knew she was just making a point. But I still hesitated. "N—no."

She kept walking with her hood at an angle, watching me. We were almost at the café. One side of her face had to be getting wet and cold. "Magica, do you have any guesses who *did?*"

"I don't know anyone. Hardly." I knew it wasn't an answer.

"Do you think it could be someone from the carnival?"

Her voice was low and kind. She was worried, just like Johann and Gloria. Is what they all thought—that my past had come back to haunt me? Maybe it had.

"I can't see why they would bother," I whispered. I don't know if she could hear me over the rain, but I meant it. And before she could ask another question, I dove for the door of the café and held it open, willing her to go inside where there was warmth and noise and distractions.

It must have been near closing time for the Pomegranate, too, but there were plenty of people still inside. It was just as bustling and bright as the day before. Like Johann had, Officer Thorn insisted on ordering a drink for herself and paying for one for me, too. This time I chose to get the cherry blossom matcha again. When Sakura gave it to me in the same plain pink ceramic mug, it fit into my hands like an old friend.

"Glacial's just finished in the kitchen for the day," Sakura told us as we stood at the end of the counter. "So she can take next shift, I think?"

She looked pointedly at Officer Thorn as she said this. Were they trying to make sure someone was always watching me? Were they *all* in on it? I hadn't told Sakura anything except my drink order. Could she see my thoughts?

Officer Thorn brushed her hand over my shoulder. It was like she'd swept everything else away. When I met her eyes, surprised, she just smiled and said, "Good luck practicing. I'm still looking into this. Don't worry."

My mouth opened, but no words came out. *But I always worry,* I almost said. *I just don't want the rest of you to worry. I'm sorry.*

But Officer Thorn was gone into the crowd, and Sakura was pulling me behind the bar.

"It's quicker if you go this way," she told me. Did she wink, too? "Just go on through the kitchen, and you'll find Glacial out back. Tell her I'm still not talking to her, will you?"

Dazed, I followed her instructions. A swinging gate at the end of the counter led me into the back room, the kitchen. It was hardly bigger than the kitchen in my rented flat. But unlike mine, its every surface gleamed, and it smelled like honey and lavender. A wooden door near the sink led outside.

Behind the kitchen, there was a shadowy porch, sheltered by the overhang of the second story. Beyond that was a little yard, mostly dirt, and then another tall building—too big to be a shed, but clearly not a business in its own right. Maybe it had once been part of the Pomegranate, when the Pomegranate had been a house, years ago? Glacial *had* mentioned a barn. To the left, at the back of the building, there were exterior stairs, but I doubted that was where I was supposed to go. Instead, I went around to the right, skirting the alley beside the café.

Wide barn doors stood open, and with a rush of relief I saw that I'd come to the right place. Glacial was inside. She'd taken off her apron for the day and was opening windows to let in some light. It had *definitely* been a barn: the entire building was one big room, two stories tall, with nothing but exposed wood beams and a brushed dirt floor.

Glacial barely glanced my way. "Not much, maybe, but at least it's got room to practice. Depending on what you want to do. I'm not familiar with acrobatics."

Shadowy dummies and what looked like a collection of sticks in one corner hinted at what Glacial was actually familiar with. I tried to take them all in, but I could hardly focus. I was too excited just seeing the beams overhead. I'd rigged up my own equipment for years, and I could tell there was possibility here.

"It's perfect," I said, propping my umbrella and coat beside the door and then walking over to her.

This time she turned to me and grinned. "Then get to it."

I'd brought my things with me this time—my bag was bursting with silks and ropes and grips. I hadn't planned out my act last night as I'd hoped, so instead I'd just brought everything—including a collapsible hoop. I decided to start off easy by playing around with that. Using an old ladder, I got up on the beams and secured the hoop so it hung in the air. It was just big enough that I could stand or sit inside it, and the system of hooks and attachments made it so that I could make it spin, too. Often the truly hard thing about hoop work is making every move look perfectly easy and still, but that also made it one of my favorite things to practice.

And it was so amazing to be in the air again! I'd done stretches and some things at home, of course. After living in the carnival for more than two decades, I couldn't just forget the old habits. But I didn't have the height and sturdy beams at home. For the first time since settling down in town, I felt that old confidence again.

I felt *free.*

We'd been practicing a while—me in the air, Glacial with her dummies at the other side of the barn. Eventually, she called a water break. When I joined her on the ground again, I could see that she'd worked up a sweat—and was surprised to find that I was overheated, too.

"Outside," she panted. "We can sit on the stairs. Come on."

Much as I wished I could keep going, I knew she was right. The last thing I needed was to get dehydrated or overheated on my first day back in the air! So I followed her as she grabbed a pitcher of water and some cups, and dashed around the building. For once, the rain outside felt refreshing.

Fortunately, though, the stairs were covered. Glacial sat on the fifth step up and gestured for me to find a seat too, saying, "Ryu extended the roof for me over the winter. Makes it nicer not having to shovel snow off the stairs."

"Do you live up there?" I asked, curious, as I accepted a cup of water from her.

She nodded. "Ryuko and Dusty, they're the carpenters in town. They cleared out the old attic and helped me insulate it."

"I hardly know anyone in town," I said, wondering over the unfamiliar names. If they didn't come into the salon, then there was a zero chance I'd recognize them.

Glacial's gaze was shrewd as she looked down. Her stair was two steps above mine. "You looked nervous with Thorn earlier."

"You saw that?" I felt my face get tight, and I set my water aside.

Glacial sipped hers placidly, still watching me. "Hiding something?"

"No," I said immediately. Too loudly. I cringed, but Glacial seemed unfazed.

"So it's not just me you're scared of," she observed.

"I'm not—" I paused. Something in the very slight curve at the corner of her mouth made me realize she was teasing. The longer I waited, the more she smiled. Finally, I confessed, "I wasn't scared of *you*. And I could never be scared of Officer Thorn. It's not that other people scare me—not exactly. It's situations I've never been in before. Conversations where I don't know what I should say."

"Say whatever you feel like," Glacial commented, as though this was common sense. But she looked interested.

"That wouldn't always be polite," I pointed out. "And sometimes—sometimes I just don't know what I feel like saying. It's like my mind goes blank."

"Like when I surprised you." Glacial thought this over. "I'm sorry about that. Saki told me later I was abrupt. She was right." After waving my reassurances away, she added, "At this point, I just assume people think I'm weird."

I got it. Where I was anxious, worried about making the right impression, she assumed she'd already made the wrong one. She was pessimistic, perhaps. "But you aren't," I said, feeling defensive for her. "You aren't weird. You're really kind. A lot of people here are."

She tilted her head as she poured us both some more water. "So why be scared?"

"I don't know. I can't help it." I hesitated: that sounded wrong. I *could* help it, maybe, but only if I made a concentrated effort. Or if I felt very comfortable with someone. "It was easier when I had Weep," I admitted.

"Who's Weep?"

I took a drink before answering. "He's my twin. We used to do the show together. We were *always* together. I've never really—I'd never been alone before I came here."

"But he didn't come too?"

"He wanted to stay with the carnival. It's fine," I said, even though I could hear how uneven my voice sounded. It *was* fine, it was just so much, so many things I hadn't talked about with anyone. "I don't mind that he stayed. We still write. But he just . . . Somehow he turned out so different from me. Even though we went through everything together."

I looked up to see that Glacial had rested her chin on her hand. She was looking out at the rain dripping from the roof above us. "You never really do know how someone else will feel about something."

I opened my mouth to argue. Wasn't that the whole point of performing—to make the audience feel a specific emotion? But my time in Belville had made me wonder. I thought of Johann, and how he'd surprised me by insisting we go to the station that morning; I thought of Sakura and Gloria, who reacted by looking out for me instead of thinking I was silly for having gotten myself in trouble. I thought about Officer Thorn, who was probably still investigating out in the rain. How did she feel about everything?

"Come on," Glacial said after a minute. "The cold doesn't get to me, but you must be freezing."

The thought of getting back to practice perked me up. "We

can warm up with round two?"

Glacial grinned. "You're on."

Eight

Golden Pun

Thorn

After I dropped Magica off at the Pomegranate, I knew exactly where to go. The post office closes about the same time as the salon. If I walked quickly, I'd find Mel.

Magica had said that she didn't think she knew anyone in town, and in some respects, maybe she was right. She'd kept a low profile. *Until volunteering for the fair.* If that was what had got her in trouble with our unknown perp, I'd kick myself right off the mountain.

Mel, who worked with Sakura to put on events at the Pomegranate, would be able to give me some perspective. Her real job was being head of the post office in town. She'd held the position for over a year now, which made her the most successful post master we'd seen in ages. As the member of the local boating club and business partner in the café, she had also quickly become one of the leading socialites around town.

And all that despite her shady boyfriend Ryuko . . .

To be fair, he hadn't caused any trouble in quite some time.

I shoved all thoughts of relationships aside as I walked up to the post office. Mel was leaving just as I arrived, coming down the stepping-stone path from the front door. I waved so she'd know I wanted a word.

"I need to talk to you about the fair," I said as I came up to her.

Her brown eyes widened. Even in her blue postal uniform and polka dot umbrella, she looked like she'd just stepped offstage. "Has something gone wrong?"

"Yes. No," I added, cursing myself. "We've had trouble, but not with the fair itself. I need you to give me a rundown on everyone involved."

"Sure," Mel said, running one hand through her short brown hair and over a pointy ear. She'd come from a family of forest elves who were once prominent in town. "Let's talk and walk, if you don't mind. I have to meet someone at Lavender's. Actually, we're supposed to be talking about fair business, so he may be able to help you, too. What is it you're looking for?"

As she fell into step beside me, headed back the way I'd come, I filled her in. Not everything, mind you, but enough for her to understand. A suspicious threat to Magica, showing up *after* she'd volunteered . . .

Mel pursed her lips. "The list of volunteers isn't publicly available, so I don't know how anyone could have found out. That's aside from us at the café and everyone at the salon, of course, but—"

"Everyone has alibis," I interjected.

Mel nearly tripped on a root as we crossed the Square. I kept telling the council to tidy up the park a bit, but they rarely listened. "You didn't really suspect one of us?"

"Just being thorough," I said. I was aiming for an airy tone, but at that moment a maple branch tugged my hood right off my head.

"Troubles of being tall," Mel said sympathetically. She was nearly as tall as I was, and far more statuesque. "Well, I can understand that you're covering all your bases. Maybe it's a good thing you found me now. You can come along and talk to Patty—he's been out talking to locals about the fair, so perhaps he's seen something or heard something of use."

The name didn't immediately ring a bell, but since we'd just hit the tavern, I kept my mouth shut. Lavender's Tavern was a popular meeting place even in good weather, and now in the drizzle it was a haven—same as the café on the other corner of the Square. It wasn't quite as loud inside, but the old wooden building held a lot more people. It sprawled across its end of the Square, the main room boasting a large fireplace on either end and a long bar in the middle. Lavender gave us both a wave as we came in. I'd already been by that morning to ask her about her other renters, so no doubt she knew what was up.

Mel led me to a table tucked near a fireplace, in a corner. We had to weave through other tables and chairs to get there. The smell of early diners' chili and cornbread made my stomach rumble. I couldn't recall if I'd stopped for lunch.

But as soon as I realized what table Mel was set on, I recalled Patty. He was sitting there, waiting for us. Half the town knew him as "the goose man;" I might've referred to him that way myself, a time or two. He'd stopped by the station when he first got to town, filing for permission to sell door to door, all that. I remembered seeing his full name on the paperwork: Patrick Rattenfanger von Helmen, or something like that. He'd said right away to just call him Patty. Usually I made a point to memorize these things about newcomers in town, but Magica's dead rat problem had erased most information from my mind.

Patty was the sort to never have problems. That much was clear even from the moment he stepped foot in the station several days before. Well dressed, slender, light on his feet, always wearing a jovial smile. Easy to be jovial when you've got a literal golden goose. In his paperwork he'd identified himself as a fairy, and he seemed to be on the short side, even for them. Mel and I towered over him. Didn't seem to bother him, though.

"Officer, are you sponsoring the fair too? What a merry band we will be!" Patty declared as we took our seats.

I turned my chair around and sat in it backwards. I had no intention of eating or even staying very long. I also did not feel very merry. "Just have some questions, that's all, Patty."

"Although she *has* been helping us recruit volunteers," Mel added, smoothing things over. "Has anyone been asking you to see the volunteer list, Patty?"

"Not a soul," he answered, looking at me speculatively. He had thick black hair and a thin black mustache, standing out against his pale skin and light green eyes. "Everyone's keen to talk about it, naturally. I went all around the lakeside neighborhood today, spreading the good word about the fair and the show."

And his goose, no doubt. I knew better than to call out a salesman on his tactics, though. Patty had gotten his permit, fair and square. I stuck to the matter at hand. "Anyone ask you about the talent show?"

"Oh, I'm only the sponsor. You know they don't tell us the important things," he said, with a friendly wink. "Even if they had been asking, I don't know what I could tell them. I do tell the kiddies to sign up, of course."

"And we appreciate that," Mel assured him. "Let's go over the schedule again, and see if anything comes to mind that the Officer might want to know."

I let them share details, thinking at any moment that I ought to just leave them to it. But I remembered Red's reservations about the golden goose, and I wondered. Of course, it made more sense to focus on one crime at a time. Especially since threats were more serious than a potential scam . . . right?

Patty took his leave pleasantly enough after confirming the talent show details with Mel. She then talked me through the rest of the fair, just in case. Just as I figured it was time to move on to the next thing, I heard a commotion at the door. Even in the raucous tavern, it was out of place. I stood at once, looking for trouble.

I'd forgotten all about Mel when Magica ran right into me.

Nine

Words of Warning

Magica

Our second round of practicing is a blur in my mind now.

The practicing itself was fine, and Glacial was wonderful. When I finally got up the courage to pass along Sakura's message—about not talking, which seemed a little scary and tense to relate—she just laughed it off. She didn't tell me what it was about, though, because that's about when we were finishing up, and suddenly the barn doors slammed closed.

The sound made my whole spine go stiff. I barely remembered to let myself down from the hoop without getting hurt. I was terrified to go too close to the doors. But Glacial wasn't scared at all.

I stood frozen, but she came storming out of her corner. She wasn't fast enough to stop the doors from closing, and she couldn't open them, either. There was another crash that must have been something heavy falling in front of the doors, keeping them closed.

And on the insides, written where we could read it now, was a message:

Stay inside where you belong

If before I'd been stunned, then I was rooted to the spot. My mind was totally blank. My whole body felt numb. I might never have remembered how to move again—that's what it seemed like at the time.

But Glacial was the opposite. She took one second to look over the message, and then she took two steps back, loosened up her shoulders, and went flying right at the door handles. I think she kicked them. Honestly, it was so fast and I was so dazed I couldn't follow her movements. She made an even louder noise than the doors closing had made. Instantly, we could see out into the gray, rainy alley again.

"I *hate* being stuck inside," she muttered. At least, I think she did. I was still standing there like a post. Glacial looked back at me and then came back and grabbed my hand. It was like she hadn't just burst through two heavy wooden doors at all.

"Come on," she said. "We're not standing for this."

I let her drag me almost out of the barn before my rational mind kicked in again. Then I was alarmed all over again. I dug my heels into the floor and tugged back on her hand. "Wait," I said. "Wait, you can't go fight him."

She whipped back and glared at me. Yesterday I'd looked at her and thought that her pastel hair and little white scales were cute. Now, she looked like at any moment she would sprout wings or horns or breathe fire. Or maybe ice . . .

"Fine," she said, after what felt like a *very* long moment. "But if I don't get to pummel the punk into the ground, then Officer Thorn does. Let's go. Now."

I'd protested when Johann suggested we go to the police station that morning. I hadn't wanted to drag Officer Thorn into this. But when Glacial said her name, this time I gave in. Somewhere inside me, a little voice said, *yes. That's what we should do.*

Glacial pulled me along, which was probably for the best. We ran through the rain without our umbrellas or coats. She towed me through the Pomegranate's back door and from one side of the kitchen to the other. As she pulled me out into the main room, behind the counter, we ran into Sakura. She was counting out the day's sales. The café was empty.

"Oh, Magica," Sakura said, as though we were behaving totally normally. "You have good timing. I was just closing up. I see Glacial is being her usual stubborn, pushy self—"

"We need to find Officer Thorn," Glacial interrupted.

That got Sakura's attention. We passed behind her stool at the register, and she turned to keep talking to us. "I just saw her walk across the Square with Mel maybe an hour ago. Why? What's going on? Magica?"

"It's nothing," I protested. But my voice was faint as Glacial hauled me out the front door.

Guiltily, I kept looking back, trying to think of how to explain it to Sakura. It turned out I didn't have to. After a moment, Sakura followed us out the door and began running carefully after us.

Glacial was practically sprinting now. I felt like a kite in the wind. I wondered where she got all her power from. She didn't weigh any more than I did. I could feel her using muscles, rather than momentum, to keep me moving. I was running, of course, and I'm not normally slow. But I stumbled over roots and slipped in the muddy grass. My body tingled all over. Was any of this real? What were we going to say to Officer Thorn? What would she think?

The moment we burst into Lavender's Tavern, none of my worries mattered. It wasn't the warmth or the happy voices. I didn't even notice that I was cold and wet. Seeing Thorn rise as we came in just seemed inevitable. It felt like the obvious answer, the choice that had been there all along. I wasn't thinking straight, or at all. I pulled my arm out of Glacial's grip and kept running.

I wasn't trying to *do* anything, exactly. I just kept running until I collided with Officer Thorn.

"Magica." I could feel her chest rising and falling. Something about her voice sounded wrong. It was me—it was my name. A stage name. It wasn't right any more. Nothing was right—

But Officer Thorn's arm was around my shoulders and I couldn't shake or flee or sink down into a puddle. So I stood through it, letting everything wash through me like the rain.

"It's alright. It's going to be alright," I heard her say. Then, over my head, to Glacial, "Is anyone hurt?"

"They would have been, but Magica said not to go fight them," Glacial said. I couldn't tell, in my strange detached place, if this was a good thing or a bad one. There was a crash as the tavern door swung open behind her, and the sound of heavy panting. Glacial spoke again, indifferently. "Oh, Sakura. The barn doesn't have doors any more."

"*What?*" Sakura's voice was breathless.

"Something happened while you were practicing?" Officer Thorn guessed.

"You couldn't—have said that—earlier?"

"Did you see who it was?" Officer Thorn again.

"You know—how I feel—about running!"

"You didn't have to follow us." Glacial must have cooled down during the trip across the park. "I didn't see anything. Neither did Magica. Except the note."

"I'm going to have to take a look at the scene." Officer Thorn sounded grim. That was what brought me out of it. I'd caused her so much trouble, after all.

"You don't have to," I said, pulling back to stand on my own.

For a moment she looked at me like I had two heads. I couldn't figure out why. Then she crossed her arms.

"I'm going, right now," she said, and I knew it was no use arguing with her. Especially when she added, "You three better come along too."

Ten

Parental Interference

Thorn

L ooking back, I'm not sure I even turned around to say goodbye to Mel. That's how it goes when there's an emergency. Sometimes, a few niceties get left behind. One lack-of-nicety I was a little needled about was Magica thinking I wouldn't investigate. It got my goat, I will admit. I walked right out of the tavern without putting on my coat, just carrying it in my hand. By the time I realized what I'd done, it was too late. The rain was barely more than a drizzle at that point anyway. I offered the raincoat to Magica instead. She may have hurt my feelings a little, I admit, but that wasn't any reason for her to be colder than she already was. She and Glacial had clearly left their outer layers behind after the attack.

I *wanted* to run right there. But as I paused to hand the coat to Magica, I saw Sakura coming out behind us. That made me think better of running. Like Magica and Glacial, she'd been through enough already. She had good reason not to like running: from the knees down, she walked on prosthetic legs. Normally you'd never know it, but I'd noticed she did prefer to take her time navigating uneven surfaces. It was about the only thing that could ever slow her down.

The four of us took several minutes to walk back to the café. Magica and I walked in silence. I could hear Sakura talking Glacial's ear off in the background, but I didn't pay much attention. I was fuming—not with Magica—with myself. There I'd been sitting warm and dry in the tavern listening to talk about Ostara pastels while the suspect had struck again!

Seeing the scene didn't make me feel any better. We went down the alley rather than through the café. Even so, there was no chance to find any clues: the rain had turned all footprints into a muddy slosh. It wasn't even worth following the Guild procedure for ground sweeps. In fact the only evidence of the perpetrator lay in chunks and splinters. Clearly, Glacial and Magica hadn't taken well to being locked inside. Not that I blamed either one of them in this case.

We took shelter inside the barn, picking our way over the remains of the doors. While I took a closer look at the painted message, Glacial pulled out a couple of chairs from one of the back corners. I turned to find Sakura sitting, looking off into the distance, while Glacial paced and Magica swayed uneasily from foot to foot.

Maybe it was the unsteady motion, or the way my yellow rain slicker went down to her ankles. But either way, whatever frustration I'd felt was gone.

"Walk me through it again," I told them. "How long were you practicing? Did you notice anyone come by?"

"You dropped Magica off yourself around four," Sakura reminded me.

"We practiced for half an hour after that," Glacial added. "Then took a break. Nothing had happened then. We went on for another half hour. It was about time to wrap up when the doors slammed."

"And you didn't see anyone?" I pressed.

Magica looked down at the ground, like she might cry.

Glacial shrugged. "I was in the back. Had to stay out of the way of Magica's hoop. She was too high up to watch the door, I expect."

Sakura reached out and tugged gently on Magica's sleeve. She didn't sit, but she did nod in agreement with Glacial.

I sighed. All I wanted to do was solve this instantly. Is it so much to ask for crime to wrap itself up? Instead, I seemed to be making things worse.

"So, it happened shortly before five," Sakura said diplomatically. "When most of the town is probably getting off work. But you think this message is related to the one yesterday? That would narrow the field of suspects a bit."

"Does it seem like the messages could be related?" I asked Magica, trying to speak more gently.

She hesitated, then nodded again. "I don't see how it could be more than one person," she said very quietly.

"True. More than one vandal in town at the same time seems unlikely," Sakura mused.

"Unless it's a copycat," said Glacial.

"Several people working together would make more sense," Sakura argued.

Between them, Magica was looking smaller and more hunched by the second.

I cleared my throat. "We'll find out soon enough. I'll take some of the paint over to Red. She might not be able to get anything by analyzing it, but it never hurts to try."

"Oh!" Magica flushed beneath her rain hood as we all looked at her. "I just meant to say, you really don't have to go to all that trouble . . . It's been so much trouble already . . ."

"Not really," Sakura beat me to it replying. "Glacial's probably *happy* she had the chance to take out those doors, honestly. And fixing the damage will give Ryu something to do, so he can stop hovering over Mel all the time."

Glacial bristled, presumably at her friend's flippant tone. "I don't like being locked in."

"We can tell," said Sakura, without looking in her direction.

"And Ryuko has enough to do building us a stage," Glacial added.

"You're not helping!" Sakura told her in a singsong tone.

"The real one causing trouble here is the perpetrator," I pointed out. "And I hate to say it, but whoever it is, they're getting braver. We need to be on our guard."

At that moment, a call came from outside. "Hello? Helloooooo? I'm coming back there!"

My heart sank. I knew exactly who was on their way. Words failed me. And while Sakura watched me with a speculative look on her face, and Glacial sulked, Magica looked around at us all and then made her way to the open doorway.

"Watch out for the wood," she called. If she was thinking that the scene was about to cause *more* trouble for someone, I could have told her otherwise.

No, there was no need to worry. My mother, wrapped up in

an old blue windbreaker and heavy rubber boots, walked right over the debris. In one hand she held an equally-wrapped up sapling nearly three feet tall. With her other hand, she swept Magica up into a tight hug.

"Hellooo!" she cried again, setting poor Magica down. "Look at you in your uniform raincoat! Gave you a bit of room to grow into it, did they? Looks like you could teach my daughter a thing or two about being prepared for the weather!"

"Daughter?" Magica echoed, following her gaze to me.

I fought the urge to hide my head in my hands. "Ma, she's not a trainee. That's Magica."

"So nice to meet you. Aren't you the cutest thing?" my mother told the woman I'd been trying to impress for six months.

"It's Officer Thorn's coat," Magica said in reply. She was gazing up at my six-foot mother with a look I couldn't quite describe. "She lent it to me."

"So you *do* remember your manners, Mina!" Ushering Magica along before her, Ma made her way into the barn and looked around cheerfully. "Hard at work, everyone? Don't let me interrupt you. I just came to find Wilhelmina. I went to the station, but you weren't there. And then that nice Red girl told me to try the café," she added to me. "Third time's the charm, I suppose!"

I sighed again. *Of course* she'd shown up at the worst possible time, days early. And *of course* she'd gone and checked in with Red. The station and the potions shop were along the same road into the Square, of course, but that bit of reasoning didn't make me feel any better.

"Hello, Ma," I said, resigning myself to my fate. "This is Sakura. She owns the café. And that other one's Glacial. And you already know Magica," I said, with a twinge of regret.

"Everyone, this is my mother."

"Call me Rosemary," Ma said, beaming without a shred of shame. "Rose for short."

"Charmed," Sakura told her, eyes alight. I could only imagine what kind of teasing I was in for later. "You're the one who was bringing in cherry boughs for the fair, right?"

"A whole wagon full," Ma assured us. "And little Cerise, of course," she added, gesturing with the sapling in her hand.

"You named the tree?" Magica leaned around her, looking at the cherry with interest. She probably thought my family and I were country oddities. I wanted to sink into the floor.

"Every living thing deserves a name, don't you think?" It was something Ma had often said as we were growing up. She winked at me as she said it now. It did not make me feel any better.

"I think it's wonderful," Magica said.

That perked me up a little.

"Please tell us you and Cerise aren't expected to cram into the station house with Wilhelmina," Sakura said, politely, with an entirely straight face.

"Mina likes her space," Ma answered, oblivious. "Usually we stay at the tavern when we come to town."

I heard that *usually* and frowned. "Haven't you made reservations? The tavern's full of people who have come to see the fair!"

"Oh, dear. With everything else, I just didn't think of it," she answered.

"It's perfectly alright," Sakura broke in. She was still purposefully not making eye contact with me. I could tell. "I think we know of the perfect solution that would be very helpful for our officer."

"Do you? You know I'm always happy to help, Mina," Ma said, looking at me curiously. Magica was still at her side, looking at that cursed tree.

"We *do*," Sakura insisted. "Turns out there is *one* room at the inn . . . An empty flat, in fact."

I glared at her. How had she known that the flat above Magica's was empty?

And yet—it wasn't entirely unreasonable.

My mother, a green-skinned orc herself, had raised a passel of children and ran a hardworking orchard, along with my father. She certainly took no nonsense. Aside from an officer of the law or an angry martial baker, she was the most likely person to scare off a criminal. And while Glacial had her own house and duties to tend to, Ma was likely to have a good deal of free time while she was in town.

"A whole flat? Sounds luxurious," my mother said. "Are you sure it'll be affordable?"

"I think arrangements can be made," Sakura said, finally glancing my way.

She looked quite pleased with herself, the meddler. But she wasn't wrong. "Come on, Ma," I said, giving in. "We'll settle things with Lavender as soon as I'm done here."

And of course, I resolved, I'd be watching the house myself.

Eleven

Flowers

⁓ꝺꝏꝺ⁓

Magica

From the moment I met her, I was in love with Rose.

Okay, I'm being a little silly. But it was so lovely meeting someone who was just so *nice* and so unbothered by everything that was going on. I could see instantly how she was Officer Thorn's mother. They were both just confident and *themselves*. And even though they bickered all the way to the tavern, it was clear that they loved each other, too.

I trailed behind them, watching the little buds on Cerise wave in the breeze as Rosemary talked and gestured. It was such a beloved little tree, all wrapped up in burlap and always carried close nearby. It sounds strange, but I was excited for it to be planted and grow in Belville. I knew it would become something even more beautiful.

Maybe that seems naive to say when at that moment I was having trouble with someone in Belville. But the threats and worries seemed childish compared to the common sense, caring attitude of the Thorns.

And Officer Thorn's first name is Wilhelmina! The secret made me feel giddy.

Officer Thorn had obviously already talked to Lavender that day, because the innkeeper agreed at once to let Rosemary stay in the flat above mine. After that, we had to walk back to the police station to get the wagon. While we walked, Rosemary told me all about the farm she lived on. Officer Thorn walked in front of us with her shoulders bunched up. Rose told me this was because *Mina* always wanted to live in the big city instead, and then Officer Thorn protested that Belville isn't a city, especially to someone who's traveled a lot like me, but I thought it all sounded perfect. How sweet, to have a family home that's been lived in for generations! How fun, to know you'll always see everyone again at holidays!

Would I ever see anyone from the carnival again? The question had haunted me since I'd decided to live in Belville. I still had no answer. But listening in on Officer Thorn's family visit reminded me how easy and natural it could be to be part of something.

It was a little different once Officer Thorn left us alone at the house, though. She said she had to follow up on some leads, but in that moment I wished she didn't.

"Well," said Rosemary. She stood with her hands on her hips, watching Officer Thorn trudge away from the front door. "Just like that girl, too stubborn to stop for dinner. Or to tell her mother what's going on, for that matter. How about you, Magica dear? Are you hungry?"

"Oh," was all I said at first. I had that odd feeling again, like I should tell her to call me by another name, a nickname maybe. But I didn't have anything to offer.

"Come inside while you think it over," Rosemary continued kindly. "You'll catch a cold. I think a nice soup and sandwich is just what we need, don't you?"

I followed her into the landing, where one locked door led to my flat and a set of stairs led up to hers. For once, I felt uncertain about which way to go. "I don't have very much food," I said, my nerves showing in my voice.

"Don't you worry about that," Rosemary said. "I always bring plenty."

There didn't seem to be any way around it. I didn't *want* there to be any way around it. I was just surprised at how easy it was, even for me, an outsider, to follow her up the stairs and feel at home.

Like mine, Rosemary's flat was already furnished, full of faded furniture and dented pots and pans. The stairs opened up to a kitchen and living room separated by a bar. I took a seat on one of the stools while Rosemary started opening one of the boxes from the wagon. I smiled as I remembered how Officer Thorn had complained to her mother about how heavy it was when she brought it up the stairs a few moments before.

"I'm not saying there's not good food in the city, mind you," Rosemary was saying as she unpacked leafy greens, potatoes, and cheese wrapped in brown paper. "But sometimes there's just nothing like good home cooking. Mina loves it every time we bring her treats from the orchard. This bread is her favorite—you'll soon see why."

"But I don't want to take it from her," I protested.

"Don't be silly, you aren't taking anything. She knows she'd better be at the table if she wants to eat," Rosemary said. Then, with a glance at me that I couldn't quite understand, she added, "It seems today she's found something more important than her mother's fresh eight grain bread."

"Eight?" I leaned over the bar, watching as she began to slice up the enormous loaf. I hadn't even known that many grains existed.

Rosemary laughed and I realized I'd said that second part aloud. But she seemed so delighted that all the mortification I would usually feel faded away. In fact, I grinned too.

"Well, it depends on how the garden's doing. Sometimes, it may be more like five or six grains. But don't you tell that to Mina. She's always been a terrible stickler for rules." Rosemary handed me a slice, pushing a ceramic crock of butter across the counter, too.

Even after months of living my new life, not having to perform or fit into costumes, I still hesitated sometimes about my food. But not now. Even cold, the bread smelled amazing, and the butter was smoother than silk. I immediately smeared some over my slice and took a bite. Rosemary beamed and nodded her head, satisfied.

"It'll be grilled cheese and creamy vegetable soup, then. Come along: you chop up that leek for me while I get the oven going."

While she had her back turned I had to quickly sort through the vegetables on the table, guessing which one the *leek* was. I settled on a long green stalk that smelled like onions. Rosemary didn't reprimand me when she turned around, so I settled into chopping while she kept chatting.

"True comfort food, this is. Seems to me you all could use

some right about now. I do wonder what's got into Mina. It's not like her to haul a box up the stairs and leave before the bread comes out. What's all this about a new case?"

The kitchen knife slipped in my grip and I wrestled with the leek. "It's my fault," I confessed.

"I doubt that," Rosemary said, without even pausing. I blinked. When she added "Go on, tell me all about it," I immediately did.

I told her about finding the rat yesterday and about the message that afternoon. I told her about coming to Belville six months before, and about volunteering for the fair. About wanting to make a new start for Ostara. I told her about Johann and Gloria and Sakura and Glacial and Officer Thorn. By the end, she was nodding along as she listened, stirring a simmering pot.

"You'll find bad actors everywhere," she said, with a sigh that reminded me of Officer Thorn. "But it sounds like you have plenty of friends to stand by you, my dear."

"Well—but—" I couldn't help protesting. Tracing my fingers across the counter, I admitted, "I wish they didn't have to. They all have better things to do."

Rosemary lifted one of her soup spoons off the counter— she'd brought her own, insisting that "city spoons" were never big enough—and rapped my hand with it. It didn't hurt at all. It just shook me up a bit.

"That's enough of that," she said firmly. "No friend wants to hear that they have better things to do than show their friendship."

"Do you—do you really think so?" I thought of Officer Thorn's face in the tavern earlier, and my heart sank. I'd made a mistake. Had I hurt her feelings?

"Of course I think so," Rosemary said. "You know, Magica, you remind me so much of my youngest when he was a little child."

"Officer Thorn's little brother?" I asked, sitting up.

"He went through a phase," Rosemary said, smiling fondly as she set a frying pan over a fresh burner. "Decided he didn't want to hurt a fly. Not even a blade of grass, mind you. It got so he couldn't leave the house. Then his sister had to go and tell him that dust bunnies have feelings too, and that he was ruining their homes when he walked on the floorboards!"

She laughed, shaking her head, but I hesitated, uncertain.

"His father and I finally sat down with him. On his bed, which by then he wouldn't leave, mind," Rosemary said fondly. "We had to have a good long talk about the ways of the world. Reminded him how everything lives, and everything dies eventually. It's not a bad thing to want to be kind to others. But it's not a good thing to let your own potential go to waste. Who are we to say that the life we were born to live isn't a good one? It's a gift, and the best we can do is live it, fully ourselves. And if that means you step on a few spiders, or need to lean on a few friends, that's all simply a part of living life. You can't forget that you're a part of a bigger world."

I tried to speak and found my throat was nearly swollen shut, choked with tears. Finally I managed, "I chose to stay in Belville because I *wanted* to live. I want to be me. But . . . being *me* . . . it changes. Sometimes I'm just not enough. I freeze. And with everything going on right now—"

"People do change. But you are always enough," Rosemary interrupted gently. "Sometimes in this life we are meant to work with others. Sometimes that is how we learn the most about ourselves."

I sat numbly watching her melt butter and slide sandwiches into the pan. The sizzle and heat was comforting, even though I'd never heard it before.

"Sometimes I freeze up," I heard myself repeat. "I wish I didn't. I wish I could handle this."

"You are handling it, dear," Rosemary said. "Some people act fast, some act slow. Mina's quick as a lightning strike when she needs to be. But some things, she takes her time and drags her feet."

"Really?" I thought this over, intrigued.

"Really," Rosemary said, with feeling. "She may not have told you, but in our family, we have a tradition. As the children grow up, there comes a time when they either choose to keep their old name, or make a new one."

"They change their names?" I shifted on my stool. What a strange thought, just when I'd been wondering about my name, too! I wondered what Officer Thorn had chosen.

"Some do. Some use the name they were given at birth. Mina took *ages,*" Rosemary told me, chuckling. She flipped one huge sandwich, then another, and explained, "I thought that child would *never* decide. Thought we'd have to send her out into the world without knowing for sure. That does happen sometimes. But finally, at the last minute, she made up her mind."

"What did she choose?"

Rosemary smiled over her shoulder. "I'll let her tell you that, dear. You be sure to ask her next time you see her."

With a happy warmth spreading through my chest, I decided that maybe I would.

Twelve

Breakfast at Mina's

Thorn

I didn't keep watch *all* night. Guild procedure states that in cases where you have no backup, it's acceptable to recruit local help. That includes Witches. And shadow witches. So keep that in mind if you ever feel like breaking the law.

I went back to Sakura that evening and had her and Trent, Belville's actual Witch, set up a protection spell over the town. Trent's a good young man, and I knew he'd take it seriously. Besides, so far our perp had preferred to act in daylight. I wasn't *too* worried about leaving things to the spell, at least for the late night and early morning.

But that's not saying I slept well.

I was halfway through eating a cold muffin and pulling on

my boots that morning when my mother arrived. She's always the first one up. I should have known to expect her.

"Ma!" I protested, when she waltzed into my living room.

"As dark and dull as ever in here, Mina!" she retorted. I knew she didn't mean anything by it, really, but I was already in a bad mood.

"I'm too busy for decorating," I grumbled.

"I'm not telling you to decorate. I'm telling you to *make a home,*" she replied loftily.

"I don't know *what* you're talking about," I muttered. But I said it mostly to my boot laces.

"I brought you some bread and butter for toast. And some eggs. Are you eating enough protein these days?"

"I have to go, Ma," I reminded her. "I have to check on Magica."

"I already dropped her off at the café for some early morning practice," Ma said, inspecting my one bookshelf. I knew she'd find it wanting, so I turned to shrugging on my coat. She went on, "Did you know Magica's one of the top acrobatic artists in the world? She's been all over Beyond!"

"I *know,* Ma," I said. Hearing about her worldliness didn't make me feel much better.

"Did you also know how sensitive and kindhearted she is?"

I turned to glare at my mother, who was smirking back at me. I shook my head.

"Listen, I'm glad you're here for Ostara," I said, as evenly as I could, "but I have an emergency on my hands. This is a stalking case. I have to—"

"Oh, I know," she interrupted, throwing up her hands with a grin. "I'm just saying. Wouldn't it be cute if—"

"Not listening!" I yelled over her.

"Good luck, Mina!" she shouted back, as I stomped out the door.

It wasn't raining this morning, but the wind had picked up. I let the breeze shake out my hair, trying to clear my head. Ma would amuse herself by baking bread or going out around the "city," so I knew I didn't have to worry about her. I could focus on Magica's case.

If only thinking about Magica didn't make it so difficult.

I'd had plenty of time to think over yesterday's events, and I'll admit I was mad at her. If she didn't like me personally, that was one thing. But if she didn't want me to investigate that was something else entirely. This was my *job*. And curse it, I wanted to do well.

Especially because, for as frustrating as she might be, Magica *was* sensitive and kind and talented. And cute.

I checked in with Trent first. There's all kinds of rules that go with being an official Witch, and one of those is that you have to live in a Hut outside of town. This made Trent's house an excellent place to start. Sort of a warm up to facing the rest of the town. And Magica.

The one problem with my plan was that Trent sleeps like a teenage boy. Or a dancing-all-night-long princess.

I nearly had to force entry through a window just to make sure he was still alive.

"I'm gonna curse you with warts and toadstools," he informed me when he finally answered the door.

At least, that *may* have been what he said. Most of it came out in a yawn. I chose to ignore it.

"The Hut's getting sturdier all the time," I observed as I invited myself into the kitchen. It had been a fixer-upper when Trent moved in a few years ago. It still only had one central room in addition to the bedroom and bathroom. But I will admit—if not to my mother—that the swept floorboards, working fireplace, and herbs hanging from the rafters were more homey than my station.

"No thanks to you trying to knock it down," Trent complained as he followed me in. "I keep telling you. If you ask me to do a big spell *the night before,* with no time for preparation, you can't expect me to get up the next morning before noon. What time is it, anyway?"

"Time for vigilance," I reminded him. Normally I might have taken a seat at the old dining table, but today I paced around it. Trent crossed his arms and watched me. His pale skin accentuated the bags under his eyes and his shoulder-length dark hair was messy. In a flannel dressing gown and fuzzy slippers he was not a picture to inspire confidence. But I did have faith in him.

"Nothing went off overnight," he said, rubbing his eyes as if he was *still* struggling to stay awake. "Sakura or I would have got you if it did."

Not to mention my mother would have done the same. That or knocked the perp senseless with a frying pan.

"Soooooo," Trent sighed, as I continued pacing, "I'm guessing you need something else?"

"We need to do more," I told him. "It's time to go on the offensive. What can you do to get me closer to an arrest?"

"I dunno," he said, scratching his head. "You said the rat's gone, right? So we can't trace anything related to that. It's kind of late to try to pick up anything from that anyway. It's best to do things within a day, or the magic fades. Maybe if the message from yesterday was intact, it would have some trace of the person's intent or feeling about it, something a spell could pick up. But . . ."

"But Glacial," I confirmed. I tugged at my ear. I wasn't mad at Glacial, not by a long shot. But we were in a tough spot. "I took the paint to Red. That's my next stop."

"Honestly," Trent began, and then stopped.

I stopped too, standing still to frown at him. "Honestly what?"

Trent bit his lip, then flung himself into the nearest kitchen chair. "I was just going to say. I don't want to be insensitive or anything, but they taught us in Divination classes that a lot of times, we already know the answer to our own questions, like on a subconscious level. So, like . . . have you just asked Magica who she thinks it is?"

I threw myself into a chair, too, ignoring the creaks as it nearly collapsed. "She won't talk to me."

"Then who reported the crimes?" Trent looked confused.

"She did," I admitted, "but only under duress. Johann and Gloria and then Glacial and your meddling Sakura had to *make* her talk to me."

"Saki isn't mine," Trent said immediately.

"Tell me honestly," I said without listening. "Am I scary? Am I a bad police officer?"

Trent pulled back, a surprised look on his face. Then, slowly, a light dawned in his eyes. A light I didn't like the look of. "*Now* I understand what Red was talking about," he crowed.

"You do not," I protested. I had no idea what conversation he was referring to, but I could guess what Red and her gossip-loving dog had said. "Alchemists only know about potions. You can't believe everything—"

"There's only one reason you would even ask me that," Trent was saying, not listening to me. "You know you're a good police officer. You're the best officer Belville's ever had. You *care* about this town. But this time you care too much, don't you? And you're scared—"

"I'm not scared," I interrupted loudly. In the silence, as Trent grinned, I added, "You really think I'm that good?"

"I've read the notes left by the past Witches. Trust me, you have a lot going for you," Trent said, still grinning.

I sighed. If only someone would point that out to Magica.

But this was no time to feel sorry for myself. One threat was one too many, and two meant a stalker who wasn't going to back down. I needed to act.

After getting Trent to promise to meet me later—after he'd cleaned himself up—to talk about protections for the fair, I set out into town. The stage and some of the decorations for Ostara were going up today, and I needed to be on hand for that. Not to mention, it was about time for Magica to head to the salon. It was those transition times when she was most vulnerable.

I strode up along the Square. The local carpenters, Ryuko and Dusty, were overseeing work on a stage. Judging by the light-hearted shouts and regular sounds of hammering, everything was going well there. Most of the businesses weren't open yet, but the café at the northern corner of the park was bustling. I decided that after Trent and his revelations, I wasn't ready to face Sakura yet. Instead, I decided to keep watch from the alchemy shop. Its windows had the perfect view on the road between the café and the salon. Besides, I needed to have words with Red.

It was still a bit early for William, so at first there was silence when I stepped into the shop. I lingered by the front windows, peering over pastel potions in egg-shaped containers.

"Ah, Officer, I figured you'd be by," Red said, emerging from her cozy chair corner with a tray of tiny seedlings in brown pots. "But I have bad news. Nothing special about that paint to report—it was just ordinary red paint, probably bought at the hardware store."

"Gives me something to look into, at least," I said. "What're those?"

"Lucky elixir seedlings," she answered fondly. "It's a special for Ostara. I was going to add them to the window display, now that there's a chance they'll see some sun."

"Don't count your eggs before they hatch," I warned her. But my heart wasn't in it.

Red gently pushed me out of her way so she could keep working. But she did pause and put her free hand on my arm. "Weather may not be my strong suit, but I'm sure everything will turn out fine."

I tossed my hair over my shoulder. "Technically, I'm mad at you for telling Trent."

"I didn't tell him anything. Did he finally connect the dots?" Red grinned. "Your anger is noted. But really, you know what Belville is like."

"Too dangerous, these days," I muttered. Glacial and Magica passed by on the road, chatting happily. I'd never seen either of them look so light on their feet.

"Yes, about that." Red pretended she was focused on arranging her display, but I caught her glance at me. "I'm not one to say we should suspect a stranger in town, just on account of them being a stranger. But I'm sure it's occurred to you that this crime is very out of the norm for Belville . . . and that maybe we should consider that someone not from Belville is responsible?"

"I was at Lavender's yesterday to get a list of all the newcomers," I said, sighing. "The trouble is, there's a lot of them. She's got nearly every room and apartment full, and most are first timers in town. I interviewed everyone on Magica's street yesterday, but that's a drop in the bucket."

"Mel is very good at promoting events," Red mused in agreement. "Well, it was just a thought. If you want some help going through the list, William should be free today. I'm busy with a project of my own."

A muffled voice floated down from upstairs. "Did I just hear you volunteer me for something?"

"It's not a bad idea," I said. Magica disappeared safely into the salon next door, and Glacial began walking back to the café. I put my hands on my hips and yelled up at the ceiling. "I hope you got your beauty sleep! We leave in two minutes."

"That's more like the Thorn we know," Red observed with a smile. "While you wait for William, I'll pack you both some breakfast."

Thirteen

New Shades

⌘

Magica

The first thing Johann said to me when Glacial dropped me off at the salon was *good for you.*

Usually Johann didn't come in until lunch time. I knew he was probably there behind the front desk because he was worried—or maybe because the rain had finally let up and we'd probably be busy. But after talking to Rosemary, and working out with Glacial, I felt like I was seeing things in a new way. Before, I would have looked at him there and felt awful. Like I was wearing shame-colored glasses instead of rose-colored ones. I know it doesn't *really* make sense, but I felt like I was taking those glasses off. He said *good for you,* and I grinned at him.

I didn't say much after that, because it turned out we *were* really busy. Everyone wanted a fresh haircut or pretty floral nails for Ostara, and all the appointments that had been delayed because of the rain came in that morning. Gloria and I were busy nonstop. When I had a question about a certain method or wanted validation about a particular cut, I'd turn and poor Gloria would be up to her ears in customers. So I had to figure a few things out for myself. But everyone was so cheerful and excited about spring that somehow, the experience was exhilarating. Like flying through the air with silks.

Maybe I just forgot, I thought to myself every once in a while. *Maybe I'm not broken and I can be happy. Maybe I just forgot, because everything in my life was so new.*

I hadn't forgotten about the threatening messages—not entirely. It's just that they felt like they belonged to a previous life.

When a huge clap of thunder sounded outside and suddenly our walk-ins ran out, it felt like a sign.

"Lunch time, at last!" Johann sang out from the front.

"Are you sure you don't want to skip straight to tea?" Gloria teased. Being busy always put her in a good mood. She cleaned off the last of the empty stations while I took a moment to finally put all my brushes and combs away. Did I really want to? Should I ask? Who was I kidding—Johann would be over the moon, and Gloria had never been anything but supportive . . .

"What do we want? I may still be able to get us some lunch specials from Third Slice. Or if you really *do* want tea, I think Sakura's featuring spring cress and egg salad sandwiches," Johann was saying.

"You *think*? As if you don't know the Pomegranate's specials by heart," Gloria said, coming to rest by the desk.

"I'd like a haircut," I announced breathlessly.

Like one person, the two of them turned and looked back at me. I was rooted to the floor of the salon. It felt good though—it felt like where I was meant to be at that moment.

"Are you sure?" Gloria asked. She'd been offering me free haircuts for months now. I'd always turned her down.

"I'm positive. I want something shorter," I said, swallowing but unable to keep down my excitement. "Something to go along with my new show. Something—springy."

"Honey," said Johann, "you couldn't have better timing."

Gloria grinned. "I couldn't agree more."

She walked back to the salon chairs, gesturing me to sit while also ordering Johann to go get sandwiches and cake. He protested at first, but when she pointed out that he'd get to see the dramatic end result that way, he agreed that it was too fun a chance to pass up. *We'll see if I even recognize you,* he told me as he waved goodbye. He looked as giddy as I felt.

I did my best to keep still for the actual haircut, though. Every once in a while, Gloria would look up and smile at me in the mirror.

"They do say Ostara is the time for fresh starts," she said.

"I meant to start over months ago," I admitted.

"Oh, I wouldn't beat yourself up about that," she told me. "Who said a fresh start has to happen all at once? Slow and steady wins the race, right?"

She was focused on another lock of hair at that point, and didn't see my eyes widen in surprise. But she was right—of course she was right. I smiled as I realized that Gloria really was my friend, aside from everything else. She gave good advice, and it felt good to think about acting on it. Leaning on people, as Rosemary had said, was not the embarrassing act I'd expected it to be.

And the first thing I need to do is apologize to Thorn, I decided. My stomach fluttered at the thought. What would it be like, to talk about something other than crime with her?

Johann came back with a huge tray full of things from the Pomegranate, but he stayed out by the desk until Gloria was done. He wanted to see the full impact, he said. So Gloria helped me blow dry my hair and then went out first to announce me like I was a model in a runway show.

And in that moment, standing in front of my friends, I did feel like I was in a show—like I was the star in my own show. It was so much more than I'd felt in my days at the carnival.

I beamed at them both and tossed my new hair. It skimmed over my shoulders and came to rest framing my face.

Johann got up, walked over, and hugged me. Then he held me at arm's length and said, "The problem now is, you're going to need new nails to match a gorgeous cut like that."

I could have cried with gratitude. Instead, I laughed more freely than I had in years.

All three of us were laughing as we perched on the front desk and ate our sandwiches, watching the rain begin again in the Square. Lightning flashed, and it made me think of what Rosemary had said about Mina.

I've made up my mind, I reminded myself. *I made it up a long time ago. This is a new me.*

Then Johann swallowed his last bite of sandwich, reached for a slice of strawberry cake, and said, "I wasn't kidding about the nails, you know."

"I was thinking," I said, taking one of the cake slices left. "I'm going to do my show with a flower theme, for Ostara. Glacial said they have people at the café who can get me flower petals, and all kinds of things. And I have an old costume, pieces of an old costume really, that I think would work."

Parts of the old costume didn't fit me any more, actually, but for once I didn't feel regretful about that. It would be fun to make it into something new.

Gloria was looking at me like she knew exactly what I was thinking, and approved. "You'll definitely be one of the most put-together acts."

"I just want to make it really nice," I said, blushing. "And that's why I was thinking, about my nails. The skirt of the costume is purple, deep purple. My favorite color."

"So obviously," Johann said, taking a handful of macarons, "we're doing your nails to match."

"Is that because of the flowers in your hair?" Gloria asked.

My breath left me. "What?"

"I noticed it when I was pruning back the viney bits," Gloria said with a shrug. To her, hair with unusual qualities—or hair that wasn't hair at all, like feathers—was nothing new. "To be honest with you, I'd never noticed the buds before. I thought it was only leaves. Maybe all that long hair was hiding them."

"Or maybe," said Johann, through a mouthful of dessert, "our protégé is blooming."

"I am not. Am I?" I leaned back and twisted over the desk to look at myself in a mirror hanging on the divider wall. I had to shake my hair out a little to see it, but Gloria had been right. In amid the golden strands and occasional slender vine, a few flower buds were showing.

Gloria was looking over my shoulder thoughtfully. "Is this really a new thing?"

"It—it is," I admitted, still half unbelieving. I'd spent years in the carnival wishing my appearance was more spellbinding, using makeup and costumes and perspective to *make* myself seem more pleasing. And now that I'd stopped all that, this happened?

"Just goes to show the importance of a good hairdresser," Gloria said behind me. Her voice was light, and I knew she was teasing.

Johann swatted her. "Stop taking away from the moment."

"Stop eating all the lemon macarons," she shot back.

I let their bickering fade into a blissful background as I turned and smiled out at the storm. No matter why it had come, the moment was beautiful. I had a feeling of being on the right track.

That afternoon, after Johann redid my nails and made me swear not to break any, I went out to take a look at the new stage. Glacial came with me. She'd come over to be my escort to the gym behind the café, and I didn't even mind. It took her three whole minutes to notice my hair. When she finally did, she said it just made me look more like myself. I could have done cartwheels.

It was still rainy, so we knew we wouldn't be practicing on it that day. I just wanted to see it, to remind myself that all this was real. Ryuko and the others had made it to be raised, about four feet from the ground, spanning between two of the tallest trees in the Square. Their branches helped to form the frame that held the curtain that hid a basic backstage area. My rigging was also already hung from the tree branches. Normally I would have climbed up the rope itself, but because everything was soaking wet, I decided to scale the tree. Its rough bark would be easy to climb. I didn't have a reason why, exactly—mostly just an excitement, eagerness to envision what things would look like while I was performing the new show.

But when I made it up to the sturdy branch that would hold my hoop, I found it wasn't so sturdy after all. Several feet away from the tree trunk, out near where the rope was anchored, a deep gash had been cut into the bark.

Fourteen

Out on a Limb

Thorn

"Can't say I've seen any rats about town. It's the birds I'm more interested in, see. In fact I'm arranging a little bird-watching trip right after the Spring Fair with some local folks. You two interested? No? Well, how about I get us another round and you can ask me any other questions you have."

Patty, number eighteen in our list of people to interview, turned across the bar to order from Lavender. In the brief silence, William leaned over to me.

"Red thinks he's hoaxing everyone," he said. "That's probably why he wanted to be a big player in the Fair."

"Red's getting mighty suspicious of everyone now that she's

settled," I muttered back. I was tired, and truthfully, I was suspicious of everyone too. We were barely halfway through our list. Anyone one of these people might have it out for Magica. And at the same time, none of them seemed to have motive or opportunity . . .

"Anyway," I added, since Patty was now chatting up a bartender, "I don't see how birdwatching is a hoax. They're real birds."

"He's been all over town trying to sell potions," William told me, keeping his voice low. "Says he's helping people make golden geese of their own."

I scrunched up my nose. Did that make any sense? Maybe I was sleep-deprived. "Let's solve one case at a time," I insisted.

Patty finally rejoined our conversation and William went quiet. But before Patty was done handing out cream sodas with violet—the tavern's Ostara special—he was interrupted.

For the second time in two days, Glacial came bursting through the tavern doors. This time Magica wasn't with her. I was off my stool before she'd said a word.

"This way," Glacial said, pivoting to lead me outside. "Are you *always* in the tavern?"

Couldn't have been too much of an emergency if she was looking to crack jokes. Still, I wasn't amused. "You always kick down doors?"

"Fair point." Glacial sped up, racing ahead of me. I didn't need her to. It was clear we were headed for the stage in the center of the Square.

As we veered around one of the trees holding up the curtains and came level with the stage, Magica came into view. My adrenaline halved. She was fine: she was just climbing down from the far tree.

"Wow, that was fast," she said to Glacial. "You found her."

There was something different about her voice. But I didn't have time to dwell on it. As the two of them began to explain the latest crime to me, my blood began to boil. It's a wonder there wasn't steam rising from my head in the rain.

By that time William had deigned to join us. I immediately put him to work. "You, go find Trent. Tell him I know he was already here this morning, but now I need him to come back. And you," I ordered, turning to Glacial, "Go talk to Sakura. Have her get Ryuko and Dusty to the café. I'll be talking with all of them when I'm done here."

The two of them ran off and disappeared in the rain. Magica and I were left alone. We'd retreated into the shallow cover of the curtain and its frame, which had probably been charmed to be waterproof. The few feet of stage covered by the overhang was dry.

I peered out and considered the offending tree branch. It was the work of our stalker, I had no doubt. But how had he gotten up there? I ran through possibilities. Some folks in Belville could fly—fairies usually had wings of some kind, and both of our witches could use magic to float if they really wanted to. Magica said she had scaled the tree, but I doubted many others would be brave enough. Especially in the rain. It was one of the tallest and straightest trees in the Square. Not even the schoolkids usually dared to climb it.

Someone must have been desperate. And desperate always means more dangerous.

"Um—Officer Thorn?" Magica's voice was soft behind me.

I turned, suddenly ashamed. She'd seen me yell at my friends and then totally ignore her, a witness and victim to a crime. "I'm sorry," I said. Something made me crouch down on one knee. I didn't think I had much right to be looking down at her. In this whole case, I really hadn't done much good.

"Oh, that's what I was going to say to you," Magica said. She reached out, touched my arm. I hadn't realized until then how cold it was outside. She went on, "*I'm* sorry. I wasn't—um, I just wasn't very nice to you yesterday. Or in general. I didn't mean anything by it. I'm still learning."

I stared at her face. There was nothing around us but deep purple shadows and silvery rain. Her hair had been cut—it framed her face perfectly. It even seemed like there were more vines in it than usual. She was smiling, shyly.

I swallowed. "Well, now, that's—that's alright. I don't mind."

She cocked her head at me. "Are you sure you weren't angry?"

"Maybe I was," I admitted. "But I'm mostly angry someone's doing these things and I haven't caught them."

Magica *hmm*ed and looked up at the tree branch. She hadn't moved her hand from my arm.

"If you don't mind," I ventured, "you don't seem very angry yourself. Or scared."

"Scared?" Her silver eyes were wide and practically luminescent. "Oh, I'm not scared about the branch, exactly. One way or another, I would have gone up there and tested the set up before the show. I don't think there was any way this would have hurt anyone. He just wanted me to cancel my act."

I can't say I agreed with this much at all. If our perp wanted the show canceled, they could have just cut the whole branch off. There didn't need to be any of this hiding in plain sight. Unless they'd been interrupted halfway through sawing off the branch, maybe.

"Are you scared?" Magica asked. She was watching me think. I sighed. "Terrified." Then I thought of Trent and his divination nonsense. Magica had sounded pretty confident talking about the stalker's plans. "Magica, are you sure you don't have any idea who did this? You're not accusing anyone. You're not going to get in trouble. But if you have any hint about it, we can use that to investigate."

For the first time she looked troubled as she gazed down at me.

But of course before she could speak, who should come bounding up but a big black dog and an interrupting Witch. A Witch who was already complaining.

"I was *just* here," Trent was saying. "Hi, you must be Magica. Officer Thorn, I'm going to start charging you for house calls."

"We met a long time ago," Magica said, stepping back from me to look up at Trent. "And technically, this isn't someone's house."

"I'm going to start charging, anyway. Upcharges for rain," Trent threatened. "William didn't tell me anything. What's going on?"

"You're the only one here with spells to keep him dry," I reminded him as I stood up. Hearing Magica speak up like that gave me energy again. Even if she hadn't answered my question.

Deciding we could talk about that later, I focused on Trent. After filling him in, I added, "Why didn't your protection spell prevent this?"

The scrawny Witch looked up at the offending tree branch, then around the stage. He shrugged. "Probably because it was already cut when I was here. I'm not saying I *know* that," he added, throwing up his hands before I could get in a question. He'd known where my mind would go. "I'm just saying, that's what makes the most sense to me. I was here just before lunch, and the rope and curtain were already up before then."

"Could be the same person who put up the rope cut the branch," William said, glowing blue as he worked magic of his own. "There's traces of practically everyone in town on this stage already. Magic isn't going to help you on this one. The carpenters'd be more useful."

Despite his exaggerations, I saw his point. "That's my next stop. But it was most likely Dusty who did the ropes, so that doesn't get us anywhere," I said.

William shook himself. "Dusty hates heights."

I took this as an interesting new fact. William and Dusty were good friends. They'd often caused trouble around town with their gossip. I knew not to doubt William's word on this, and that opened up new possibilities. Had Dusty and Ryuko gotten a volunteer to put up the ropes? Someone unknown so far?

I had William and Trent go over the stage again just in case, and then left them to weave a more powerful protection spell. Magica hurried along after me as we headed to the Pomegranate next. By then, Sakura had assembled everyone I needed. Sometimes her insight came in handy. And from the fact that she already had a pot of strong rosehip black tea ready for me, I assumed that she'd noticed I hadn't asked them to trudge out in the rain. Working with her was smoother than corralling her ne'er-do-well boyfriend, Trent.

For his faults, I do love him. But herding Witches is worse than herding talking cats.

Ryuko and Dusty weren't much use. In order to finish work before the rain, they'd recruited about every volunteer around. Even Mel and the sponsors for the fair had been in and out, checking on the progress. William might have been right with his *everyone in Belville* comment after all.

They *were* definite about who had put up the ropes and curtains, at least. It had been Glacial, running out to help during a break from the café.

She was sitting there next to Magica, listening in to this conversation. When I turned to glare at her, she shrugged one impertinent shoulder. "No one else wanted to go up that high. I'm not afraid of heights."

I crossed my arms. "Are you afraid of stalking and endangerment charges?"

"Officer Thorn!" Magica protested. "It wasn't Glacial. She was *with* me when we got the message yesterday."

That didn't strike me as an airtight alibi. She could have slipped out for a minute and done some writing. And there was plenty of paint around the Pomegranate, which seemed to be in a constant state of construction and improvements.

But I didn't want to argue with Magica. In the end, I sent Ryuko and Dusty back out to the stage to check on Trent and anything else that might have gone wrong. I sent William back to Red with instructions to check out the paint shop lead, since I wouldn't have time. Sakura sent everyone out the door with free chocolate cupcakes decorated with pastel eggs. Glacial sent me a dirty look and refused to give me any, on the basis that she'd been the one to design and bake them.

She did give a full half dozen to Magica, though, who tucked the box under her arm and left the café at my side.

And who should meet us at the door but my mother.

"I just ran into William, and he filled me in," she said. I had to wonder, *how?* He'd literally left two minutes before us. But such was my mother's power to involve herself. "Have the two of you even thought about dinner?"

I ground my teeth. "Ma . . ."

"Nonsense," she replied cheerfully. "Come along. Mina, I assume you'll want us to stay safely tucked away in our flats?"

"Yes," I grumbled. "And this time, I'm staying, too."

It wasn't totally out of procedure. Normally I'd have preferred to stay out and finish my interviews. It would have been more in line with the Guild handbook, but I had to admit I was run down. And doing the interviews just seemed to be spinning my wheels. Maybe if I set myself up in Magica's flat and Magica up in Ma's flat, then the perpetrator would save me a lot of time and come to *me*.

I did feel a little like I was breaking the rules. Not a comfortable feeling, but needs must, I reminded myself. Besides, Magica didn't seem bothered in the least by my decision. She and Ma walked ahead of me, chatting about the quality of bread from Ginger's Bakery and how many grains could be found in "the city."

My stomach rumbled. I hadn't eaten all day, and Ma's bread was always delicious.

Still, though, some rules couldn't be ignored. When we got to the house, I sent Ma upstairs and offered to help Magica gather up some of her things. She let me into her flat without another thought. It wasn't anything unusual, especially for one of Lavender's rooms. But there was a lot of art on the walls—interspersed with far too many windows, I decided.

"I left the carnival thinking I'd totally start over," Magica told me as she disappeared into a bedroom. I stood in the living room, surveying as much as I could. "But then they sent me boxes of my things a month or two later. All my old costumes and pictures and everything. Do you mind if I bring some of my practicing things? Just because we didn't get to run through our routines this afternoon."

I winced at a *we* that included Glacial, the little baking ruffian. But of course I wasn't going to say no.

"We'll figure something out," I assured Magica. "Are you sure you don't mind having to share a flat with Ma?"

"Are you joking?" Magica poked her head out to look at me. At first she looked like she was actually worried I might be setting her up. Then she smiled. "I don't mind if she doesn't. She's been really sweet. And honestly, it gets quiet here alone. I know I said I wasn't scared about the branch, but I really do . . ." she hesitated, thinking, then said finally, "I really do appreciate how everyone wants to help. I want to *let* people help."

"We've always been willing to help," I said awkwardly. Magica disappeared again and there was the sound of clothes rustling. When she came back into the doorway, I cleared my throat and said, "Magica, I'm sorry that—you seem to—since you came here—I'm sorry it seems like you haven't always had people to let help you."

"Oh." She blinked, and stood there considering it, an old canvas bag in her hands.

"I know it's not my fault and maybe not my place to apologize about it," I added. "I'm sorry if we've been making you think about it lately. Does—does that make sense?"

"I think it does," she said slowly, smiling a little at me. I sighed with relief. She continued, "You're right, you don't have to be sorry. But I think it's—it's really kind of you to notice. And to be sympathetic about it. And you don't have to worry. Maybe it was unusual, or even unfortunate, the way things were at the carnival. But in the past few months, I've been realizing that everyone was only doing the best they could. It's okay, really. It just makes me especially glad I could end up here."

My breath caught, but I was determined not to cry.

Fifteen

Practice

Magica

When Officer Thorn and I walked into Rosemary's apartment, I had to go first. I was a little nervous to, but it would have been really awkward to stop at the door and wait. When I came in she smiled at me, in a very knowing way that kind of reminded me of Johann. It made me blush, but at the same time, I relaxed. I know it was only meant to be a temporary shelter, but it felt a lot like home.

Rose already had a bunch of ingredients out on her kitchen counter. I hadn't realized how dark it was outside, or how late. My stomach rumbled, and I think Officer Thorn's did, too. It made me want to turn around and grin at her. Instead, as soon as we set down my things, Rosemary told us what to do.

"Mina, you sit," she said, directing her daughter to the stool I'd sat in last night. "You drink that whole cup of tea before I let you into my kitchen. You look dead on your feet. She's no help to us," Rose added to me. I was still surprised she could talk that way about Officer Thorn, but I knew that she was teasing. I smiled, and she handed me a knife, saying, "You, my dear, will work on your chopping skills. Do you know which ones the potatoes are?"

She steered me toward her box of vegetables, and I felt my jaw tighten. But Officer Thorn, who had dutifully sat across the bar, set down her tea mug and said "Ignore her, Magica. Teasing is how the Thorns show you you've been accepted. But they have terrible timing," she added pointedly, frowning at her mother.

"The stalker isn't banging down our door, now, are they?" Rose retorted. "You need to let yourself relax, daughter."

"It's okay," I said. My shoulders dropped as I said it, and I realized that actually, it *was* okay—it was more than okay. "It's funny, actually. Potatoes are easy, but yesterday she asked me to find a leek. I had to guess which one it was. I thought you didn't notice," I added, looking up at Rose.

"Oh, dearie, mothers have eyes in the back of their heads," she told me. "And when you sliced it up into little sticks instead of rounds, I knew you'd never had one in your soup before."

Officer Thorn raised one perfect eyebrow at me. I giggled. "I did wonder why it was so difficult," I admitted. "But once I'd started, I couldn't stop."

"Leeks aren't a big favorite on floating carnivals, I'm guessing," she said. When I laughed out loud, she finally leaned over the counter and chuckled too.

"It's never too late to learn something new," Rosemary told us, smiling along. "Magica, you can chop the potatoes into round slices this time. Mina, finish up your tea already. I need you to grate this cheese."

She turned to search through the kitchen cabinets, banging and clattering and finally pulling out a square ceramic pan. Even as I set up my cutting board, I couldn't contain my curiosity. "What are we having tonight?"

"You girls are making taters and gravy," Rose said. "I'll make a salad and slice up some fresh bread."

"It's not really called that," Officer Thorn told me. "That's just what we called it when we were kids. It's potato slices baked with cream and cheese."

"Sounds wonderful," I admitted. Suddenly, chopping up potatoes was much more exciting. I'd never had mess hall duty at the carnival, and I found it fascinating how ingredients could come together into something new. "Oh, and we can have Glacial's cupcakes for dessert!"

"She probably poisoned mine," Officer Thorn said into her teacup.

"No, she said you don't get any, remember? So only Rose and I will eat them," I answered, grinning.

Rosemary turned from the oven behind me and patted my shoulder. "There you go, dear. You'll get the hang of it yet."

Officer Thorn stuck her tongue out at her mother, but I thought secretly she looked pleased.

After that, cooking dinner was a blur. There was only room for me and Rosemary behind the counter, so Officer Thorn stayed on her stool, grating up cheese that turned out to be from the family's goat. I got to be in the middle while they traded family stories and told me about their holidays, when Rosemary and everyone would descend on Belville to see Officer Thorn, since it was hard for her to get the time away from Belville. I had certainly seen how she was connected to everyone in town, and knew exactly who to ask to do what. She was so clever about things like that, even when she was angry or sad. It reminded me of some of the star performers I'd met over the years, though I didn't tell her that.

I did run through my show for them after dinner, though—at least, as best as I could. Officer Thorn found a ladder in one of the closets, and she held it propped at an angle for me, counterbalancing my hoop with the weight of her foot. I couldn't swing or flip, but it was enough height to hang freely, so I could show them some of the flower shapes I'd strung together in an act. Rosemary said it was the most impressive thing she'd ever seen, and how did I manage not to tangle myself up in the hoop? I admitted that I used to get tangled up often, when I first started out. This made her laugh and tell me how Officer Thorn and her siblings used to challenge each other to tree-climbing and rope-swinging into a nearby stream.

"That was a long time ago," Officer Thorn reminded her mother, as I got down from my hoop and started winding up the rope.

"And what do you have to say for yourself now?" Rosemary asked her. "I'll bet you haven't even commented on Magica's lovely new hair."

I shook it out, a little self-conscious, and a little pleased. It *was* lovely, and surprisingly fun to have a new look to get used to. One of the vines brushing my cheek.

"We were busy," Officer Thorn protested. But as she pulled the ladder back, she leaned on it, looking down. "But it *is* nice, Magica. Really nice. Did you do it just for the show?"

"It was time for something new." I hesitated, thinking of

telling them both about the flower buds, or maybe even asking Thorn about her name.

But just at that moment, Rose remembered the cupcake box still sitting on the counter. Officer Thorn made a joke, asked her if she really thought she *desserted* cupcakes, or something like that but more clever, and it was nice just to go along with the flow. I felt like there would be time later. Even later, when I went to make up my bed in the spare room, I felt like these moments might go on forever.

Sixteen

Ships Passing

Thorn

A noise woke me up in the middle of the night.

After we'd stayed up on the second floor all evening with the lights on, I'd realized that any stalker worth their salt knew where Magica must be. So in the end I'd decided to sleep on the couch on the second floor, rather than be a whole floor away. It eased my mind a little, even if it wasn't easy on my back. That couch definitely wasn't made for tall and heavy people.

It was a footstep that jolted me upright. All the lights were off. It had to be after midnight.

And the sound was coming from inside the house.

They tell you in training to embrace your strengths. Orcs

and half-orcs like me might be good at force and volume, but I know better than to attempt stealth. I hopped off the couch without trying to be quiet. Let the stalker know what's coming for them, I thought.

But the next sound I heard was a very faint *"eek!"*

"Magica?" I asked, hesitant.

"Oh, Officer Thorn! It's just me," she answered.

I have good vision in the dark, and when she spoke, I could locate her easily enough. She'd come out of her room and into the kitchen. There wasn't anyone else nearby—no one threatening her. I sighed, rolled my shoulders, and walked over to the counter. "Late night snack?" I asked, trying not to let on how unsettled I'd been.

"Something like that. I'm sorry if I scared you," she said. Apparently she'd seen right through me. "I was hoping I wouldn't wake you up. Although I know the whole point of you sleeping out here was to keep watch, sort of, so I guess that was silly on my part. Do you mind if I turn on a lamp?"

"Go ahead," I said. I settled on to a stool as she snapped her fingers at the light over the stove, and the charm inside flickered to life. The pale yellow glow made her fuzzy pajamas and pullover sweater look orange.

"I get cold at night," she said, tugging at the collar of the old sweater.

"Don't let Ma see that," was all I could say. "She'll insist on getting Pa to knit you a new one. He spent a year recovering from a back injury and in that time we *all* got new sweaters."

Magica chuckled. "I think that sounds nice. I don't even know how long I've had this one."

"So," I said, turning away from her wardrobe, "you couldn't sleep?"

She hesitated, thinking it over. I didn't mind waiting. I liked how she thought about things before answering them. Made me feel like I was getting a real answer.

"I couldn't sleep," she agreed at last, "but it's not because I was worried, exactly. I know you, and Rosemary too, and everyone, are doing their best, and nothing will happen tonight. But there's just so much going on. So many things to think about, and—and some to be excited about, even."

I couldn't read her face as she looked at me. But I knew what she meant. "We've all been busy," I agreed. "Especially you."

"Would you like some?" she asked. "I—I was planning on making warm milk. Maybe with some cinnamon, if I could find any."

"I would," I said, adding, "please."

She turned to rustle around in the icebox, then in the spice drawer, and then among the pots and pans. Eventually, once she'd assembled everything, she said, "I know it must seem strange—maybe I *should* be more worried."

"I don't think you're strange," I said, watching her measure out two glasses' worth of milk. I thought of saying more, but decided to stick to the case. *Focus.* "At the Guild, we talk a lot about how everyone handles things differently."

"The police guild, you mean?" Magica didn't look back at me, but she nodded along. "Yes, it's—something like that. I compartmentalize. I've been doing it so long most times I don't even think about it."

"I could see how you might have to," I told her quietly. "For performances, I mean. You'd have to focus and not let anything else distract you."

"I never thought about it exactly like that, but I think you're right," she said, glancing back at me before striking a match and lighting the stove. "But sometimes it sort of—bubbles over. I get anxious and can't *stop* being distracted. Not by things that matter, but by really little things." She laughed a little, shaking her head. "I can't help but think I must have been so erratic these past months. And you, everyone here—all my friends—you've just been nice about it."

"I don't think you're erratic," I said.

"To be honest, maybe I've been hiding my thoughts so you *wouldn't* think I was erratic," she admitted without turning around.

The words were a weight lifted off my chest. If that was what she was worried about, it was no trouble at all! I struggled to figure out what to say without sounding inappropriately joyful. "Changing your mind is a normal part of processing an event," I said, falling back on language I'd been taught. "They tell us that at the Guild. And I think it's true. It's not your thoughts that make you erratic. It'd be something in *you,* deeper than just thoughts or feelings. What really matters is what you choose to do with those things. That's what makes us who we are no matter what else goes on."

Magica had been stirring the milk in the pan. Her stirring slowed, and slowed, and finally stopped. She walked over and leaned on the counter. Her hands were only inches from mine.

"I'll tell you what I think," she said. "I haven't been trying hard enough to see who *you* are, deeply, like that. I've been too selfish and stuck in my head. I haven't wanted to tell you my fears about what's going on because I didn't want to admit my past had caught up with me. I didn't want you to see the past me. I want you to see the new me."

"I don't mind," I whispered. "It's still *you.*"

"Right." Magica was whispering too. "I'll tell you everything, tomorrow. But first you have to promise me not to get hurt."

I hesitated. Not a lot of people worry about someone twice their size getting hurt. It wasn't something I usually thought about for myself, to be fair. But maybe that was why I was so adrift on this case. Magica had talked about seeing *her*—I hadn't been seeing myself, either.

"You can think about it," she said, pulling back.

"Magica—" I started to protest.

"Oh, and that's the other thing." She paused, turning to smile at me. "You could call me Maggie, maybe? And sometime, you'll have to tell me about your name. Your mother told me about how you thought about it for a long time. I like Wilhelmina. I'm not sure I've always liked Magica, but it was a good stage name. But for my friends, now, I've been thinking, maybe it would be nice to have something more informal. I know people don't usually get to pick their nicknames, but, well, I *am* trying to be new, and . . . and *you* did, didn't you? In a way."

"Maggie," I repeated, wholly distracted. "You can call me Mina."

She smiled at me again and started to step closer—but at that moment, the milk boiled over.

Seventeen

Don't Blink

Maggie

Technically, I didn't do anything wrong.

Actually it felt like I was doing something right. I went to bed with my warm milk and I thought about Officer Thorn—about Mina. I thought about how she would handle things. She knew exactly how to cut to the heart of something. What could I do, if I was like that?

I stayed up even later thinking, and I had to scramble that morning. Mina and Rose walked me to the salon through a hazy mist. It was the day before the fair, the day before Ostara and new starts. It was time for this to be over.

The salon was busy, but this time we managed to close for lunch on time. I volunteered to walk with Johann to the Third

Slice to get everyone pizza, but while he was ordering, I slipped away for a minute. It was only meant to be a minute—after all, like basically every business in Belville, the Third Slice is right on Market Square. There wasn't very far to go.

I walked right up to the stage, and hopped onto the solid wooden boards. Then, almost as if by accident, I walked over to the tree that had once held up my rope. The damaged branch had been cut away. I stood against the trunk I'd scaled yesterday, wondering if I was right or wrong. The temptation to dwell on all my doubts and questions was strong. But I had to stay alert to the outside world.

I didn't have to wait long.

"You know you shouldn't be here," said a voice from behind the tree.

I looked straight ahead. My jaw was tight, but I willed it to be firm and determined rather than afraid. "Leave me alone, and I'll leave you alone."

"You only have one option here," he replied.

"I won't say anything. I'll swear it."

"No one trusts the word of a carnival junkie. I don't know why I'm even bothered about you. Even if you did say something, no one would believe you."

"I know someone who will believe me," I said, clinging to the fact. I did, didn't I? I knew she would. Even if I'd never tried to speak up before, I knew that if I did now . . .

"Who? Your scaly little friend? Don't make me laugh," the voice crowed. "You're nothing but an outcast here. Six months, and this is all you've made of yourself? No one will take your word over mine."

"They will," I protested, almost shrill. I gulped deep breaths, trying to sound calm. "They would. If I told them, they would.

But I won't, I promise. All I want to do is perform and then—then go home."

"You have no home here. I'll run you out before you can even think of returning to the stage."

This really wasn't going the way I'd hoped. I gasped again, trying to remember what I'd wanted to say. "All I want to do is go on with my show. I don't care what you do. I was never going to say anything."

"Spare me," he snarled. "I'm the one who doesn't care. You're the one who's sniveling."

"Just leave me and my friends alone," I said. I was—I was pleading. I hated it.

"You won't have to worry about them when I'm through. If you know what's good for you, you'll never show your face around town again. And you can forget all about your precious show!"

I couldn't stand it. What should I do? Shout? Turn? Run?

I was rooted to the spot.

It had been quiet for a very long time when, once more, the rain began.

Eighteen

Crisis of Faith

Thorn

Of course, I wasn't expecting her to go and tell me everything while my eavesdropping mother was around, offering people breakfast and chattering about sights. And a person does have to work, secrets and stalkers or no. But for once I could admit that after I dropped her off, what I wanted most was just to turn around and talk to her.

Maggie.

It was perfect. And I was more certain than ever that she knew something important. Once we sat down and put our heads together, we could get this thing solved, then go out and—

There were two options on my mind, and I have to admit, neither one was very lawful.

I swung by the station to make sure there were no messages, then turned around and headed straight for Red's potion shop. I expected a report on the paint lead, but as I walked up to the back door, I heard voices.

I paused. Red's was usually open at this hour, but she never allowed customers into her lab, which was right behind the back door. So who was there?

"—*should tell her,*" a voice was saying as I put my ear to the keyhole.

"*I tried, but she won't listen!*" That voice was definitely Red's.

"*But she's the one who should be doing something.*" That voice was male. In fact, it sounded like Trent. What was so important that he was up early, and speaking coherently to boot?

"Thorn reporting!" I announced, in my old Guild fashion, rapping at the door. Enough secrets!

"Ah, Officer, we were expecting you," Red said as she let me in. She was in her lab coat and goggles as though everything was normal. But the two witches shuffling behind her lab table gave her away.

I glared at Trent and Sakura, who stood next to him. So she'd been the first voice. And while she could pull off a perfectly guiltless expression, her boyfriend couldn't. I *knew* they'd been talking about me.

"What should I be told?" I demanded. "Am I right in thinking this doesn't have to do with my paint?"

"Well—" Red dragged out the word.

"Does it at least have to do with the stalking case?" I insisted.

"With *Magica's* case," Sakura corrected. She leaned toward me, putting her hands on the table in front of her. "Let's be clear about a few things first, okay, Officer?"

"Let's," I agreed, fuming. I kicked Red's lab bench aside and took a seat, stubbornly waiting for the rest of them to follow. No one was worming out of this conversation.

"First of all, let's say something we all agree on," Sakura said brightly. She always did like a storm cloud hanging over a conversation. "Repeat after me: Magica has a stalker."

I thought it was ridiculous, but I wanted them talking. I started off normal. "Magica has a—"

That's where I faltered. I couldn't say it.

Trent coughed.

I crossed my arms. "What is the point of this?"

Red was sitting next to me, but even she wouldn't quite meet my eye. "Well, you haven't quite been yourself . . ."

"Our concern," Sakura broke in, "is that normally, you are our upfront and clear-sighted Officer Thorn. Wouldn't you agree?"

I narrowed my eyes at her, looking for the trap.

"And now," she explained, smoothing her hands over the worktable, "you're not facing up to a few important facts. And your stubborn ignorance is getting in our way."

"Getting in the way of justice," Trent added, agreeing.

I looked over at him, hurt. He knew me well enough to know a comment like that would get my attention.

Red cleared her throat. "We're not trying to pick on you, Thorn. We're your friends. It's just that—well, exactly what Saki said."

"I don't know what you mean," I declared. I did, but I didn't want to. And I still didn't see how it was relevant.

"Okay, let's start farther back, then," Sakura suggested. "At what point did you realize you were in love with Magica?"

I faltered. "I—I don't think that matters."

Red gave me that look. "Would you say the same thing to me if we were trying to solve a case about Luca?"

"You and your bookseller are different," I said. They all kept looking at me, and I felt caught. "They are," I protested. "Red and Luca are dating. You, Trent, and Sakura— you're—something. Sort of dating, close enough. I'm not saying I want to know," I added, putting up a hand when Trent opened his mouth. "But that's all *different.* You know you like each other. I and—I mean, there is no *and,* and that's that. It doesn't count. There isn't an 'us.'"

"But there's still your feelings," Sakura said gently. "Don't you think they could still be getting in the way?"

I shut my mouth. She'd got me there. I remembered what I'd said to Maggie the night before, that thoughts and feelings don't matter as much as choices in the end . . .

And here I was with a really beautiful feeling. And I'd chosen to ignore it until it twisted up all my other thoughts and feelings.

Poisoning the well—that's what Ma would call it.

Maybe Sakura and her dratted intervention committee had a point.

"It's not that you've done anything wrong," Trent added in the silence. "It's just that you've been, well . . ."

I smiled wryly. "Erratic?"

"Something like that." He grinned back, ducking his head.

I sighed. "Okay. You got me." I knew what they wanted, and with another deep breath, I reminded myself I was strong enough to do it. I said, "Yes, fine. I'm in love with Maggie. She asked me to call her that, but she didn't say anything about *you* all, so keep your mouths shut," I added, feeling much lighter.

"And . . . Maggie has a stalker. It makes me feel powerless and scared and *awful.* And I've been a mess about it, I know. I've been . . ."

"On your back foot this entire time, largely ignoring the friends and experts you usually conscript into service?" Sakura supplied cheerfully.

I turned to look at Red instead. "Would've thought you'd be glad to have a break, the way you and that dog of yours go on," I said sheepishly.

Red's mouth quirked up, and she reached out to squeeze my hand. "Maybe under normal circumstances. But I really think something is wrong here, so we couldn't just sit back and wait."

"Tell me what you've all been up to, then," I said, addressing all of them. "Go on. I know Trent isn't here and dressed at this hour just to harangue me about my love life."

"Ask Glacial if you want to hear about haranguing," Sakura said, with a rather evil little smirk on her pretty face.

"It's the birds," Red said, shifting into a more professional manner. "This whole golden goose thing. Have you heard the latest rumors? People are being told they can 'create' golden geese of their own. They're going to go out after Ostara and I'm pretty sure the plan is to catch a bunch of birds that they can try to—to change into 'golden' versions."

"Patty did say something about birdwatching," I admitted, tugging at my ear as I thought about all the little things I'd overlooked. "But doesn't it all seem far-fetched?"

"It *is,*" Red said firmly. "It absolutely is. There's no such thing as a diet or potion or regimen that makes a bird lay golden eggs. Don't you think an actual alchemist would have discovered it centuries ago if there was? This is all a bunch of lies, and furthermore, it's going to turn into some kind of animal abuse."

"And as for the citizens of Belville," Sakura added, "they're being seduced by this siren song of free money."

I set my elbow on the table, thinking this through. Trent nudged Sakura. "Nice turn of phrase," he mumbled.

She looked up at him through her lashes—and then crossed her eyes. "Trust me, as a shadow witch, you see lots of this kind of thing."

"I agree with you that it's happening," I said finally. "But I don't see what you want me to do about it. He came in with all his paperwork—everything was in order. And since I haven't heard him make any promises—and if you don't have any *proof* of the promises—I can't just chuck him in jail."

"That isn't *quite* what we were thinking," Red said, glancing across the table.

Trent and Sakura grinned identical villainous grins. "We have a plan. And don't worry—it might help Magica, too."

Two birds, one witchy trap. The idea had appeal, I must admit.

We'd finally finished talking over the finer points of their plan when Johann burst in and told us that Maggie had disappeared.

Nineteen

Face the Music

Maggie

If only I hadn't frozen up.

I kept standing there, thinking about it. All the words I hadn't managed to say were stuck in my throat. I hadn't done it. I hadn't been enough.

But you are enough, Rose had told me.

But could I really believe that? Especially after how I'd messed things up?

At some point, all the shame and regret washed over me, and I broke. I jumped away from the tree trunk and started running. I ran until I was all alone.

It was Sakura who found me. She materialized out of a cloud of black and purple sparks. If I hadn't been so entirely consumed in my own misery, I might have taken fright and bolted again. As it was, she landed lightly on the hillside beside me and all I could do was stare at her, numb.

"I had a feeling this was where you might come," she said. Turning over her shoulder, she looked out at the empty lake. Below us, the boats and dock were abandoned, sitting quiet in the rain. The town faded away to the right.

"How?" I asked. "How do you know me?"

"Oh, it really isn't difficult. Most people wear their secrets on their sleeves. Allusions no one is supposed to follow up on, a left-behind past on a carnival ship that was once docked on this very lake . . ." Sakura smiled as she turned back to me. "Haunted, are you?"

I didn't know what to say. I tucked my knees up under my chin, and sighed.

"But you don't need to worry," she went on, unbothered. "Everyone else is busy, and we'll let them figure things out for themselves. I'll sit with you awhile. But I'm not sitting on wet grass." She took a scrap of fabric from the pocket of her yellow dress, and black magic sparkled from her fingertips, then all around her hand, her arm, and the space between us. I blinked and the fabric was gone, and instead I sat inside a cozy little tent.

"That's better," Sakura said, joining me on the quilted floor. "Nature is a lot nicer when you can view it in comfort, don't you think?"

We were both now looking out into the rain, out at the lake. I bit my lip. "Sakura, I—"

"Saki," she corrected placidly.

". . . Saki," I said, timidly. "Um—"

"Mind," she interrupted, "if you tell me I don't have to do this,

I'm going to revoke your side of the tent."

My breath caught. At first I wondered how she'd known yet *another* secret, a private conversation. But then I realized that this, too, was probably easy to tell. She was reading me like a book. "I feel horrible," I said, since she probably could tell that, too. "Everyone's been so supportive, you included. I wish I was just *better*. I wish I could leave everything behind."

"Yes," Saki agreed, absently toying with the lacy white tights covering her legs. "There's a lot of things we all wish we could snap our fingers and heal from." When she snapped hers, both of her calves shimmered for a moment, revealing the wooden prosthetics beneath the magical spell.

I caught my breath. She'd said she hated running, but I hadn't realized *why*.

"But healing isn't like that," she added. "And besides, sometimes the new *you* you're working to create is even better. It's worth waiting for." With another wave of her hands, her cute tights and prim shoes were back, free from mud and blemishes. She leveled a look at me, waiting until I met her eyes. "It's worth *working* for."

"I know," I admitted. "Gloria, Rosemary, Mina—they've all shown me that I can be better."

"And I'm sure they were very nice about it." Saki paused and smiled before cocking her head. "Magica, do you want to hear some advice that isn't as nice?"

Well, she was probably the most powerful witch I'd ever seen. No one I'd ever performed with or encountered could transport themselves blocks away, levitate, create a tent from nearly nothing, *and* maintain a powerful glamour spell in one afternoon and make it look like nothing. Who was I to turn her down?

And—I realized it as I nodded—I *did* want to hear it, nice or not. Something in me was ready for a hard truth. Something to break through all the doubts.

"There are a lot of ways to end up a victim," Sakura told me, holding my gaze. "A victim of circumstance, of tragedy, of someone else's abuse. It's unfortunate and unfair, and victims deserve sympathy. They need *nice* in order to move forward. *Nice* shows us where the light is. It's normal to need that, and your gratitude is to your credit."

I swallowed hard, reminded of just how desperately I appreciated the kindnesses I'd found.

"However," Saki went on, "with light comes darkness. You have to choose, over and over, which to stay in. Someone or something might cast darkness over you. You have to choose to move into the light. You can not stay where you are and wait for the world to fix itself for you. Do you understand?"

"I know *exactly* what you mean," I confessed. "When I dwell on something for too long, it's like I'm taking the old injury and doing it over and over again, to myself."

"So you know what you were doing by isolating yourself, then," Saki said. "Why did you choose to come here instead of finding Officer Thorn?"

"I—um—" I sighed. "It didn't feel like a choice. It felt like I had to stay on my own and figure out what I did wrong."

Feelings and thoughts. But *choices* make us who we are . . .

"Saki," I said, looking up again, "how do *you* deal with fear?"

"That's the fun part," she said, smiling at me. "You drag it into the light."

Twenty

Coffee Talk

Thorn

When the shadow witch *poof*ed into nowhere instead of helping us search, that was one thing. But when she *poof*ed back with Maggie at her side, I was fit to burst.

We'd been searching for an hour, turning Belville upside down. The two appeared right on the stage in the center of town. That shadow witch knew *exactly* what she was doing.

Before I could murder either one of them—or, more likely, arrest them and just throw everyone in jail until the cursed Spring Fair was over—Sakura pulled Magica and me both into the Pomegranate Café.

I don't get pulled around very often. It was impressive, I'll admit. My first burst of temper passed pretty quickly. By the time we were at the café door, all I felt was relief, and my knees were weak. By the time we'd been deposited on a couch with cups of tea, I could almost talk again.

"I'm really sorry," Magica began. The moment she started talking, the rest of the café and its afternoon rush faded away. "I told you I was going to tell you everything, and then I did the opposite. I made the wrong choice."

I sighed heavily, reminded of what my friends had told me earlier. "It isn't my job to pass judgment. I haven't been at my best with this case either."

"I think you've been perfect," she said. The look in her eyes was sincere. "I want to try again, and make the right choice this time. Let's go over everything. If you don't mind?"

I hesitated, unsure exactly what to say. In the silence Maggie sipped from her pink matcha bowl, then smiled and held it out to me. "You should try some," she said. "It's really good."

But I knew I'd better take things one step at a time. "In a minute," I promised her. "For now, I need to focus on being a police officer over being a . . . a friend."

Her silver eyes shimmered, and the vines tangled in her hair trembled. But then she set aside her mug and sat up with a small smile. "I understand. Do you want to ask questions, or should I just try to tell you the whole thing?"

"Tell me everything you think is relevant." I didn't trust myself to come with, and stick to, the right questions.

"Okay." Magica took a deep breath, closing her eyes for a moment. When she spoke again, her voice shook, but quickly became resolute. "You asked me if I knew who would leave a dead rat at my door, or the message on the barn. I do. At least, I've had a feeling about it from the beginning, and after today,

I'm pretty sure. It's not anyone from the carnival—at this point, I don't think they'd care if I shared any old secrets. But there *is* someone in town I know from before. We were never friends, but I think he's worried I could still tell things about him that would—that would be bad for whatever he's trying to do now."

I did my best to stay neutral. I had to use every trick in the Guild handbook. "Go on."

She nodded and tucked her hands in her lap. "It was several years ago. The carnival was docked at Oasis, the biggest of the desert islands. It's a really big port, and there's a lot of tourists there, so the captain had us stay there longer than usual—I think it was a whole season. But towards the end of it, there was trouble. People, tourists, disappeared. The local police thought it might be something to do with us—with the carnival. But we had no idea what was happening. It was like a bunch of people, strangers to each other, all walked out of their hotels overnight.

"And then," she said, steadying herself with her arms stiff against her knees, "one person who had been missing showed up at the port. She floated in on a raft made from pieces of ship-wrecked boats. She was terribly sunburned and dehydrated. They had to wait a day or more before she could even speak.

"She told the police that she and a group of strangers had gone out on a trip. It was supposed to be just like any other tourist attraction. But once they'd gotten out on the boat, their guide told them something was wrong. He said the boat needed repairs, and that he could get them flown in, but only if they paid him lots of money to pay the pilot. Everyone pitched in. But the pilot never showed up. Then their guide took them to one of the deserted islands, a tiny unmapped island. He said he'd leave them there and go get help. But since the boat was too dangerous for tourists and everything on board it technically belonged to the tour company, they had to pay him for any supplies they left behind. So they paid him whatever they could, and then overnight, he left. And that was the last anyone on the island ever saw of him. When they realized they were abandoned, they sent out the one woman to find help. The police were able to rescue everyone else. But there was never any record of the boat tour, no tickets sold or anything. And of course the tour company name and the guide's name had been fake.

"And besides, by then he had a lot of money. He got away."

I resisted the urge to tug at my ear or bury my face in my hands. "Nature of the trips they were taking?"

"Birdwatching," she said, confirming my fears. "And—it *is* him. I knew him then. We all did. He was—he was advertising with our show."

"Can you confirm for me who it is, just so we're clear?" I asked.

"It's—his name here is Patty," she said, clearly shivering over the name. But it had to be done. "It was something else in Oasis. And he didn't have a mustache. But I recognized him—honestly, I recognized the goose first. He brought it round the salon, the first day he was in town. He saw me and I know he recognized me right away, but he didn't say anything then. And neither did I. I was so worried . . . I didn't want to try to say something, only to find out no one would believe me. After all everything I'd hoped about living here—I didn't want to feel that way again."

I took a long sip of my coffee, letting this sink in. The con, the trip, the dratted *birds*—and now he was planning to take folk from *our* town out into the woods, too. It tallied with everything Red, Trent, and Sakura had suspected. And here I'd ignored them all. I'd spoken to the man myself, several times, and not given him another thought.

But, I could practically hear my mother telling me, *you certainly know how to pick sharp-eyed unofficial assistants.*

"I'm sorry I didn't say anything sooner," Maggie added softly. "I worried maybe I was wrong, or he'd changed. Then I thought maybe I could fix it on my own—that maybe that would be best, not to involve anyone. I wasn't sure what he'd do to any of you. So I tried to talk to him this morning, but—it didn't go the way I'd hoped. He just said—he said I shouldn't perform, and should just be quiet, because no one would believe me anyway."

I looked over at her. She'd hugged her arms around herself now, and was looking at the floor.

"I believe you," I said. "I believe every word. Believe it or not, this confirms something Red and Saki have been trying to tell me from the start. But even if no one else had sniffed it out, I'd still believe you now."

Her face lightened, her jaw dropped, and then she leaned forward and threw her arms around my neck. "Oh, thank you! But oh—I'm sorry—I probably shouldn't have done that, it's not very professional," she added, backing away with a blush.

"It's alright," I managed. "We can switch gears now. Friends?" I offered her my hand to shake.

She looked at it for a moment, then up at me. "Partners?" she suggested instead.

"Sure." That one was even harder to get out, and I had to hide my expression with an impromptu hair toss. But she clasped my hand warmly, and I knew we'd taken a step forward.

I was probably blushing myself, but I did my best to stay focused. "You know," I said, clearing my throat, "a lot of people would believe you. Gloria, for one. She wouldn't have kept you on at the salon if she didn't."

"When you say it that way, it sounds obvious. Sometimes I'm just too in my head," Maggie said, smiling.

"I've been trying to stay out of my head," I admitted. I wasn't sure it made any sense, but Maggie laughed.

"We'll have to meet in the middle, then. You know, when I first got here, before she told me she was aromantic, I had the start of a crush on Gloria. Guess it just goes to show I kind of have a type," she said.

I nearly spat out my coffee. "What?"

"Nothing. How's your coffee? Do you know the person who's helping with drinks today?" Maggie said in a rush. I knew she was trying to distract me, but it was for the best. I wasn't sure if I did or did not want to know what she'd meant.

I glanced across the café at the shop counter. Our couch was tucked into the front corner, farthest from the register and slightly hidden by a staircase going up to the balcony. But I did recall Sakura saying she had an "assistant" today for the fair. I could see glimpses of him: a tall, tan man with antlers rising up from forest green hair.

"I haven't met him," Maggie continued confidentially, "but from something Glacial said yesterday, I think *she* knows him really well. She was really annoyed at Saki for asking him to come in."

My coffee was good, so I saw no reason to complain. And Maggie's lifted spirits and apparent closeness with Sakura made me smile. "Listen, speaking of meddlers. Red and Saki are trying to get me to agree to set a trap tomorrow."

"For Patty." She seemed less scared now to say it. "I want to help."

"You've already helped," I reminded her. "Soon as I leave here, I'll put in a wire to the Oasis station, and see what they can give me. But for now, I still don't have the kind of proof I'd need to lock him up and get a trial. Even for the things he's done in Belville, to you, I don't have solid evidence."

"And the fair is tomorrow," Maggie prompted, eyes on mine.

"Right. Which is where Saki proposed we catch him." I drained my coffee and set it down. "I have to admit, I don't normally go in for these dramatic confrontations. It's not, strictly speaking, Guild procedure. However . . ."

"It's a con," Maggie put in, resting her hand on my arm as she leaned in. "It's like a performance. He gets everyone to believe him. So to get everyone on your side, to help with the arrest, you have to show them who he really is."

"Exactly," I agreed. "I don't want people banging down the station door demanding I let him go. Especially if they think he's going to make them all rich as soon as he's free. So. Do you think we should take part in Red and Sakura's scheme?"

Maggie's whole face shone. "Yes. Let's come up with a plan."

Twenty-One

On Stage

Maggie

I've never been so excited about a show.

I was pretty nervous, too, of course—that was a more familiar feeling. But when the morning of Ostara arrived, I knew it was time. I could feel it.

Apparently, Red had devised some kind of potion that would reveal the golden goose as just a *goose*. Mina and I went to the potions shop early to pick it up, and then I scaled the tree beside the stage and hid. Just in time, too. For once, it was a sunny morning, and people were coming to the Square with breakfast still in hand. We'd have a full house, that was for sure.

Glacial and Mel were on stage below, setting up for the talent show. They'd taken my name off the list so that Patty would think he had won. But really, we were all planning for an interruption before the show even began.

The announcements started right on time, at ten. By then, it seemed like everyone in Belville was standing in the audience. Most held steaming cups from the Pomegranate or fresh breakfast sandwiches.

"Good morning, everyone, and happy Ostara!" Mel was the presenter, since Saki was busy with the café and Glacial had probably said she didn't want to. I hadn't spoken much to Mel myself, but she was obviously the perfect choice: she was confident, smiling, and very cute in a flower crown. Even without a magicked microphone, her voice carried over the park. "Vendor stands are open now for those who need a gift or snack, and the egg hunt will begin at twelve sharp. But for now, why don't we kick off our celebration with a little talent show?"

Everyone clapped: they'd known this was coming. It was on all the banners.

"Our very first act is also a generous sponsor of this fair, so be sure to make him feel welcome. I'm sure many of you are familiar with him already . . . Not to mention, familiar with his golden goose!"

As the crowd cheered, Mel bowed and gracefully walked off the stage. She knew what was coming, and went to join Trent backstage.

When Patty came out, I had to resist the urge to gag. Everything about him seemed fake, from his smile to his shiny green coat to the tired goose sitting on his shoulder. It was hard to believe I'd let someone like *him* keep me from speaking. He had a gaggle of chickens with him, birds he was supposed to turn into 'golden' versions right before the crowd's eyes.

I gave my ropes a quick tug and got into position.

He started talking, and honestly, I didn't listen to a word.

I swung down out of the tree, potion in hand, and on the backswing when I was sure of my aim, I dumped the whole thing all over all of them.

At first, people clapped. I think they thought it was part of the act. But then it *worked.* The goose shook its head, and flecks of fake gold went flying. Patty's coat and hat were splattered with it. Plus, he was wet. When he looked up and saw me, it was clear he was *mad.*

I hadn't realized that he could fly.

He leapt into the air, brilliant green wings sprouting from his back. He was a *fairy*—I hadn't known that before. We'd had one in the carnival for a while, an animal tamer who could hide her wings and then make them appear at will. Patty did a somersault in the air, amazing the crowd and swiping his hat off in a bow, like this was all planned. Then he flew up to where I sat on my swing and turned to address the crowd.

"It's not the gold on the outside that counts," he told them. "It's the gold on the *inside!* Yes, my goose is only a plain, normal goose. And yet look what I have managed to accomplish! You, too, could have all this and more, my friends. You could leave your worries behind and be soaring through the sky!"

Fairies fly like bugs. I've always thought so. They can dart around without warning. Patty darted behind me and made like he was going to push my swing, like it was just another part of the act. I reacted without thinking. I flipped backward on my seat, kicking his hat off his head before he could get out of the way. Then I swung down, holding on to my seat with my hands, and leapt to the safety of the wooden frame holding up the stage curtain.

There was scattered clapping, like people still weren't sure what to think. I watched Patty more carefully this time. I was standing above the curtain now, and I felt reasonably secure. I knew Mina and Red and the others were waiting, but the goose potion hadn't gone the way they'd planned. He hadn't admitted to anything yet.

"Sometimes, fortune just isn't with us," he was telling the crowd. "Sometimes, it can feel like fate is *conspiring against us.* But I'm here to tell you that you can take your fate into your own hands. You can turn your fortune around!"

He darted right at me, like he really was going to knock me off the frame. Alarmed, I ran along the curtain toward the right side of the stage. It was good that in Belville I'd been walking everywhere, keeping up my leg strength. I was barely fast enough to make it to the end of the curtain before he caught up. I dove and swung onto another tree branch, this one a little lower, a little closer to safety.

Again, a few people clapped, but this time they were murmuring too.

I twisted myself up so that I could crouch on the branch, waiting. Patty had returned to center stage, catching his breath.

"You see, you have the power," he said. "You can do anything you set your mind to. And you'll have the money to support it! That's my guarantee to you!"

"No!" I shouted.

I wouldn't have thought I'd be loud enough to reach the crowd. But I swung forward through the branches and leaves, running out along a thick branch so that I could face them. The sunlight struck my eyes and I almost slipped. I'd lost track of where Patty was. "It's all *lies,*" I cried to them. "The only act here is *his* act. The words he keeps feeding you. None of them

131

are true! He twists everything. He's hurt people before!"

"I'd never hurt a fly. It's people's *jealousy* that hurts them!" he replied. His voice came from above me. I swung down, then around the branch as he followed me. While he got stuck in the leaves, I darted back along the branch toward the stage. Climbing down would have taken too much time. My friends had come out from behind the curtains and were shouting. I vaulted back to the curtain frame and turned to shout too.

"He's a wanted criminal! He's only here for your money. Everything since he's come to town has been a sham!"

And there was Mina, her voice even louder. "I have a warrant for your arrest from Oasis!"

"Ah-*ha!*" Patty rose up over us, crowing. The whole Square fell quiet. "You see!" he yelled. He was too high for me to reach. "You see how they conspire against me? Think of what they aren't telling you. They say I make things up, but they can make up lies just as easily, can't they? Especially because this supposedly impartial officer of the law is in *love* with this acrobat!"

There was a gasp. I registered the words, but I wasn't listening to them. I was rooted to the spot . . . because I was waiting for a very specific chance.

"Nothing you say can change the fact that you've extorted, cheated, and even *murdered* people all across Beyond!" Mina.

"Isn't that convenient? I'm sure you'd love to make an arrest, just on this *stranger's* word. Where's your impartiality now?"

His feet were dangling as he yelled down at the stage.

"Where's your honor?" Someone else taunted. Trent.

Patty made a sound of pure rage. He ducked down lower, as if to face his accusers. He must have forgotten all about me. My chance had come.

I leapt.

I kept my muscles taut, trying not to swirl through the air. If I lost my grip I might go flying. He flailed and screamed above me. I clung to his shoes. *Steady, steady.* Even in the chaos, I could hold on. Although, I realized, I hadn't thought beyond this point . . .

That's when purple sparks of magic curled around us both. *My favorite color.* I relaxed a little. Then tendrils of black joined the purple, and Patty and I were pulled down, down onto the stage.

"Thanks for that," Trent told me. His eyes and hair sparkled purple, but his grin looked exactly the same, lopsided and boyish. "I couldn't catch him with him flying all over the place like that."

"You sure you weren't just waiting until you had help?" Saki looked much more in tune with her deep black magic. "We heard the commotion all the way from the café. What'd I miss?"

"Patrick Rattenfanger von Hameln," said Mina, in her most official voice, "you are now under arrest."

Twenty-Two

All the World

༶

Mina

I t didn't go *exactly* as planned. But then, arrests rarely do. That's why it's one of the golden rules of the Guild handbook to always be prepared.

Patty cursed me out all the way to the station. It was nice that Trent came along: I had someone to roll my eyes with. And a witness in case I got a little too tempted to get Patty back for all the danger he'd put Maggie in.

The best revenge is justice, as we say in the Guild.

And there was no doubt we'd get that. The Oasis station had sent a full report in that morning, along with some related reports from other towns. And after seeing that Patty *could* fly, perfectly well, I felt confident he could have sawed up Maggie's branch. Despite all his talk of alibis, flying meant he could get around town quick, too—he probably had just enough time to vandalize the Pomegranate's barn door after he'd left Mel and me. After we'd told him Maggie would be going ahead with her performance.

There'd be no flying or magic in the station, though—the jail cell is specifically warded against that. Once Trent and I put him safely away, we could relax.

I felt like a weight had been lifted from my shoulders . . . except for one little comment Patty'd made.

"Do you think she noticed?" I finally asked Trent as we walked back toward the fair. "She must've, right?"

"I dunno," he said, scratching his head. "She seemed pretty distracted. Probably lining up her jump."

And what a jump! I sighed and shook my head. It had been amazing, sure, but it had also been *much* more unsafe than planned.

"Don't feel bad," Trent said, punching my shoulder. "We've all had worse."

"You have not!" I protested.

He started ticking things off on his fingers. "Red got knocked in a well, you once threw Dusty in jail, Gloria survived a creature attack, Daisy got injured in a dragon fight, Saki and I literally fought a—"

"Wait up!" I interrupted. "The dragon thing was not my fault. And neither is people running off on their own and getting into trouble. What exactly are you trying to prove here?"

"Just that we all love you, and we'd do anything to help you out," Trent said. This time, he wrapped one lanky arm around my shoulders. At least, as far as he could reach. Before I shook him off, he added, "And maybe it's not such a bad thing if you let her know."

I guess I have a type. The memory made me blush.

"I gotta go help out at the café before Saki and Glacial murder each other," Trent said as we neared the Square and he headed for the Pomegranate. "See you later. Think about it!"

"Keep the peace! No more room at the station!" I shouted back. But a moment later, I realized there wasn't any need.

In the Square, the talent show had resumed and was in full swing. Glacial was wrapping up her act as I came up. An elaborate staff-fighting display, from the looks of it, which would only add fuel to the rumors that she was an ex-mercenary. I sighed to myself. That baker was trouble.

Still, I had to admit she'd been a good friend to Maggie so far. I tried to dwell on the positive as I bought a cherry danish from the bakery booth. Then I turned and ran right into my mother.

"Ma!" I brushed crumbs from my uniform. "Where have you been?"

"I had a front-row seat, of course," she said cheerfully. "Did you think I was going to miss it, after hearing you girls stay up planning it all night?"

"It wasn't all night," I grumbled.

"You were wonderful," she continued, ignoring me. "Both of you. If I hadn't known any better, I would have thought that *was* the plan!"

"I don't *plan* to put my friends in harm's way, thank you very much," I said. And I took a big bite of my pastry for good measure.

Ma gave me a knowing look. "I remember you as a little girl, leading your brothers charging into the woods. Never mind that they were all smaller than you. Some lessons take a long time to learn."

I knew what she was trying to say. *Not everyone is as powerful as you are.* And yet . . . hadn't Magica proved today that she *was* as powerful as me, if not more so? In her own way, of course. I wouldn't have caught Patty if it weren't for her.

"Speaking of," said my mother, with her usual unnerving tendency to read thoughts, "I believe it's Maggie's turn on stage. Shall we go see?"

The question was rhetorical. I was already on my way.

It was an incredible show. It was perfect. She looked beautiful, like a fairy queen, scattering flower petals and making the crowd *ooh* and *ahh* in amazement. All throughout her hair, purple flowers blossomed and moved with her. It was exactly what the fair needed.

Ma whooped and clapped twice as loud as anyone else, and then she leaned in to me with a smirk. "I'm off to inspect the rest of the stalls, then. Did you know there's even a hen-painting station?"

I raised an eyebrow, unsure if she was just trying to get my goat. "Shouldn't you be guarding the cherry sapling?"

"Cerise's dedication will be the finale, this evening at sunset," she reminded me primly. "And the cherry branches are all around. Do open your eyes, dear. And don't be afraid to open your heart, either."

I opened my *mouth* to protest, but she'd already melted into the crowd.

So, as the kids' acts started, I did look around. I'd been so focused on the criminal and the trap that morning. But now that it was over, I could see that Sakura and Mel had really outdone themselves. Blooming cherry boughs and ribbons in white and yellow hung from every tree. Many of the shops around the Square had chosen to decorate their doors and windows. The vendors ran booths under striped pink awnings, and music floated from the air.

All told, it was a lovely day in Belville.

Maggie and Mel both helped the kids run their musical acts and performances. I stayed until it was over, and lingered even after most of the families had left.

"I thought I saw you in the crowd," Maggie called, smiling. She slipped out from behind the stage curtains and crossed over to me, sitting at the edge of the stage with her feet dangling. "The egg hunt is happening on the lawn, so the stage is free until the dedication this evening. Want to sit with me? You must be tired of standing."

I pulled myself on to the stage and sat next to her. For lack of anything else to say, I focused on the schedule. "They really had to limit egg hunts in town," I told her. "One year, the competition got so fierce someone unleashed a giant chicken made entirely of sugar on the crowd."

"That sounds frightening," Maggie said, eyes wide and almost laughing. "And messy."

"Come to think of it, that's one crime we never solved," I mused.

Maggie grinned. "I guess maybe we should be glad today only involved a goose. And a pack of normal-sized chickens."

"And a very out-of-line fairy," I added, more serious. "Maggie, look, I—"

"It's okay." She interrupted me by putting her hand over mine. "I know it isn't what any of us expected, but it worked out, right?"

"It did. You might be called on to speak at the trial," I said, reverting to the most basic facts.

She kept looking at me, her head to one side, as if to say, *is that really what you want to talk about?*

"I don't suppose," I said at last, "you gave much thought to anything he had to say."

"None," she said at once. Then, with a shy smile, she added, "That's a little hard to do, you know. I do keep remembering the mean things he said. But I remind myself that everything he said was obviously untrue. People did believe me, and the truth did win out."

This was good to hear, but it wasn't entirely what I'd meant.

Maggie ran her fingertips over the back of my hand, looking out over the fair as she added, "If there was anything that he had said, that you thought *was* true, you could tell me now . . . I mean, I've forgotten what *he* said, exactly, but I'd definitely be paying attention if *you* thought it was important."

"And true," I added.

"Right. And true," she agreed.

I cleared my throat. When she turned her eyes to mine, they looked exactly like moonlight, and her face was still framed by beautiful flowers. "It *is* true, Maggie. And I guess everyone's been able to see it except me. I didn't want to admit it and scare you away. But I can see that you're not easily scared," I said, and she giggled. "So . . . I *do* love you. I've loved you since pretty much the moment we met."

"Huh." She paused, and then her lips curved up in a gorgeous smile. "Well, you might have me beat. I've only *known* I loved you since two nights ago, when you said to call you Mina. But I guess it might have started earlier than that. You've been such a steady presence in my life, even when—even when everything else was on the ropes," she said modestly.

If I hadn't loved her already, I would have definitely fallen head over heels right then. I reached out. "Partners?"

Maggie looked down at my hand. She took it in one of hers, but she wrapped her other arm around my neck. With the sweetest look on her face, she echoed what I'd said yesterday. "Sure."

Cheers went up around the park as we kissed. Turns out all the world's a stage . . .

. . . And that's not such a bad feeling, when you're in an act with heart.

Epilogue

Sakura

The Ostara Fair was another great success for the Pomegranate Café team, if I do say so myself. I found the dedication of Cerise particularly moving, but maybe that's just because it was the first quiet moment I'd had all day. And that's not because the café was full of customers, mind you. Between Trent catching a criminal and then Glacial bickering with Hunter, I barely got a moment's peace!

Let it never be said that I hold a grudge unduly. However, I *do* know when to take a step back and give myself a break. Within two days I saw Maggie once more, when I decided to treat myself to some salon time.

Johann sent me straight back to Maggie, who looked *much* more radiant since Ostara, if I do say so myself. She was standing straight and smiling, and purple flowers were still blooming in her golden hair.

"Too bad I can't ask for the same cut *you* have," I told her, teasing, after we'd exchanged hellos.

"I could probably get flowers to stick in your hair with some of our new super-strength hairspray," she offered, grinning. "But I guess that's not quite the same?"

"Not at all. Besides, I like my look." I settled into the chair and leaned my head back. As she wrapped a towel over my shoulders and prepared to wash my hair, I kept chatting. "I do wonder what your secret is, though. How did the flowers happen? Or are they a normal springtime occurrence?"

"Not normal, not for me," Maggie told me. "It's never happened before, anyway. I wrote to my twin to ask him about it, just in case. But I always thought it was just leaves, you know, like trailing willow branches."

"Not everything is in a name," I observed.

She chuckled. "You're right. And I don't mind them at all. I think it's . . . fitting."

"It absolutely is, Maggie," I said, my eyes closed, smiling to myself. She'd given me permission to use her nickname when we sat talking on the hill before the fair, something I'd been very touched by. "And it will make quite the statement at the trial."

"Did Mina tell you? It's next week," Maggie said.

"I hadn't heard." Officer Thorn had *not* given me permission to use her first name, but I was still gratified to hear it.

"She says the evidence just keeps coming. It's basically overwhelming," Maggie said, running her fingers through my hair expertly. "There's no reason to think he'll get out of it. Still, you know Mina."

"Very careful," I agreed, "once she's finally opened her eyes and taken a look around."

"What was that?"

142

"Oh, nothing. I'm glad to hear all the loose ends have been wrapped up."

Behind me, Magica chuckled. "Shouldn't you say, all the loose feathers?"

"You, my dear, have been spending too much time with Officer Thorn," I said, without opening my eyes.

"Probably," she agreed. "And it's lovely."

Equally lovely was the chance to hear such even, happy tones in Maggie's voice—and the excellent trim she gave me. I walked out of the salon feeling quite pleased with myself. I might have even started humming.

That was, of course, until Trent ran up behind me.

"Saki," he panted, his hand on my shoulder. Honestly, you'd think a Witch as good as Trent would use magic to get around once in a while, but he seems to enjoy roughing it. "Saki, we have a problem."

"What problem?" I asked, reluctant to snap out of my post-event planning high.

"It's Hunter," Trent said. "He knows."

I stopped in the road. There were only the trees in the Square nearby to listen in, and doubtless they've heard much juicier stories. "Hunter knows a lot of things, Trent. Don't let him unnerve you. He's just testing you. Besides, wasn't he leaving today?"

Trent nodded, but did not look reassured. "Already on his way out. But Saki . . . *what about Glacial?*"

I turned and looked at the Pomegranate, my beautiful café.

What about Glacial, indeed?

About the Author

Elle adores happy endings, fairy tales, and above all, learning new things. As a historian and educator, she believes in the value of stories as a mirror for complicated realities. She currently lives in New Jersey with a grumpy tortoise and a three-legged cat.

Find more stories set in Belville at ellehartford.com. And while you're there, sign up for Elle's newsletter to get bonus material and free short stories!

And *stay tuned!* More stories from the Pomegranate will be on their way soon. In the meantime, if you loved this one, Elle and Sakura will be eternally grateful if you left a review!

Also by Elle Hartford

If you loved your time in Belville, and you like mysteries, you're in luck! The Alchemical Tales is a cozy mystery/cozy fantasy series centered around Red, the alchemist with the nosy dog. You can get a set of free prequel short stories by signing up for my newsletter, or you can check out the first novel in the series:

Beauty and the Alchemist

In this magical mix-up of fairy tales and murder, Little Red Riding Hood solves the mystery at the heart of Beauty and the Beast . . . *What does it take to overcome a curse?* Alchemist Red and her friends will need all the help they can get to solve a crime and uncover the truth!